Sharna
of
Rocky Bay

Sharna
of
Rocky Bay

By
Alice Mertie Underhill

TEACH Services, Inc.
PUBLISHING
www.TEACHServices.com • (800) 367-1844

Facsimile Reproduction
As this book played a formative role in the development of Christian thought and the publisher feels that this book, with its candor and depth, still holds significance for the church today. Therefore the publisher has chosen to reproduce this historical classic from an original copy. Frequent variations in the quality of the print are unavoidable due to the condition of the original. Thus the print may look darker or lighter or appear to be missing detail, more in some places than in others.

Copyright © 2014 TEACH Services, Inc.
ISBN-13: 978-1-57258-285-9 (Paperback)
Library of Congress Control Number: 2004108040

TEACH Services, Inc.
PUBLISHING
www.TEACHServices.com • (800) 367-1844

CONTENTS

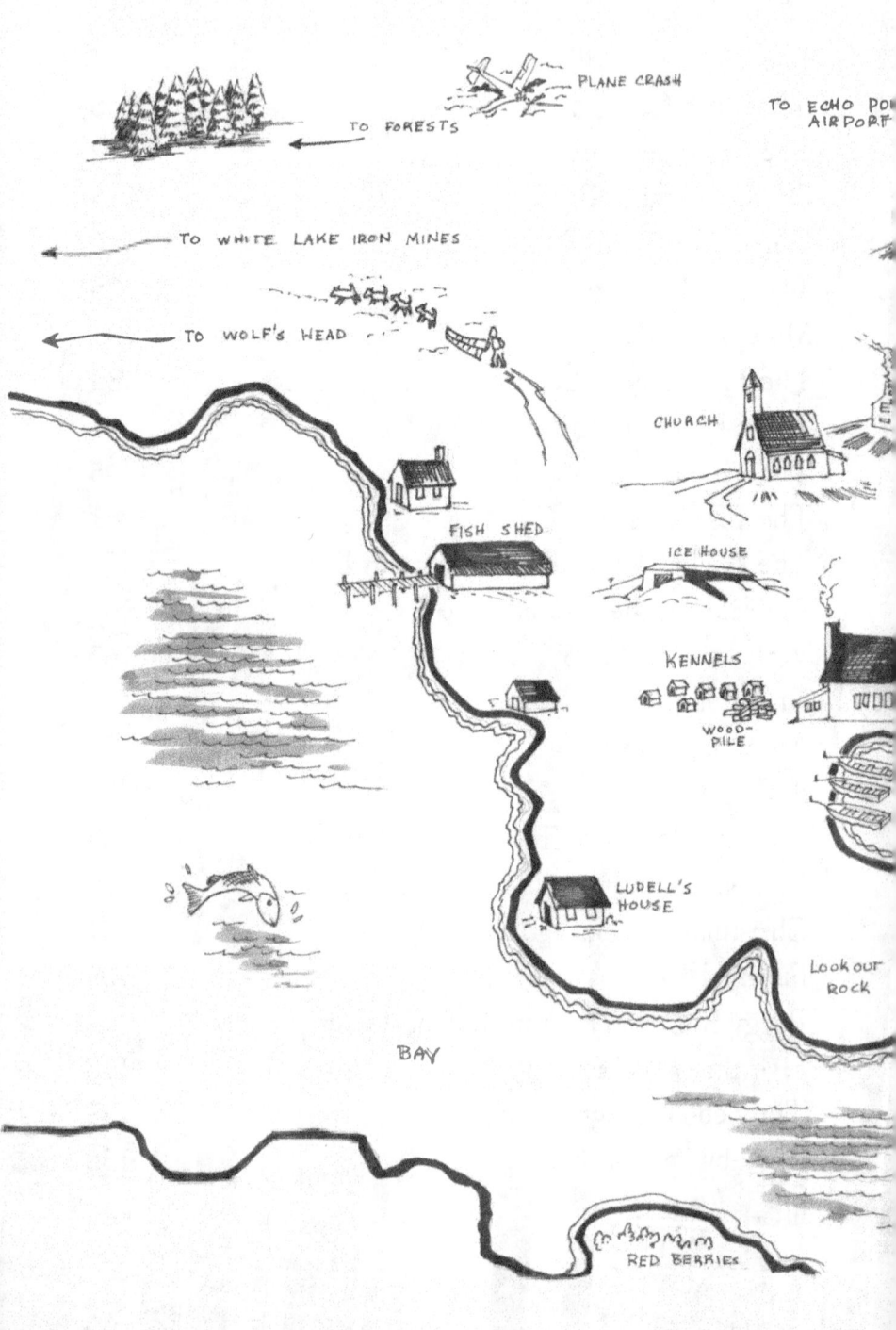

TO CRYSTAL ACRES HOSPITAL

UNCLE TOM'S HOUSE

NURSING STATION

BOBBY'S HOUSE

HILL

PARSONAGE

TOMMY'S HOUSE

BOBBY PATCH

GRANDFATHER'S
(WHERE TEACHER BOARDED)

COVE

POLE

WHARF

HARNA'S HOUSE

MUD

UNCLE REX

POST OFFICE
(AUNT MINNIE AND
UNCLE JOE)

TELEGRADH
OFFICE

N
W E
S

Village of Rocky Bay

Sharna and Lolo sat in the bow of the boat shivering, while Don rowed. The wind was blowing, and the waves splashed against the sides of the boat.

The Morning Call

"AH-O-O-O, o-o-o, o-o-o!" It was an eerie sound. Sharna pulled the heavy woolen blanket up over her head. She did not like the noise. Was it only the wind whistling around the house, or could it be wolves? The girl was not fully awake, for it was early in the morning, and quite dark. It would be two hours before the sun would peek into the little square window of the upstairs room.

"Ah-o-o-o, o-o-o, o-o-o!" it came again, followed by a series of yelps and sharp barks.

"Oh, it is just dogs!" decided Sharna, turning over in bed, being careful not to awaken her little sister, Lolo, who was sleeping peacefully beside her. "I wish they would not 'owl so," sighed Sharna, "but maybe they are 'ungry. It takes a lot of scraps and fish 'eads to keep 'em satisfied."

She cuddled down, trying to go back to sleep, but the dogs continued to howl. The wind whistled around the house. It always blew in the Far North country, and sometimes it rocked the little wooden buildings until the boards creaked. Sharna was glad the house was built up on the rocks, instead of down in the soft marshy land.

It was beginning to get light in the east. Sharna could hear mother moving about in the kitchen downstairs, putting wood in the stove and filling the teakettle from the water barrel. Soon she would call the children to come down to breakfast. This would be another busy day with plenty of work for Sharna. All the children in the village of Rocky Bay were used to hard work. The older boys cared for the dogs, went fishing, helped to build boats, went for wood in the winter, and hunted with the men for large game in the forest. The younger boys brought water from the springs, did errands for mother, or snared rabbits and birds for food. The girls helped their mothers in the house. Even little Lolo, who was only six, would be expected to do her part.

The dogs were still howling. It seemed that all the dogs in the village of Rocky Bay had joined in the weird chorus.

Suddenly there was a noise in the other bedroom where the boys slept. Sharna listened. Someone was putting on his boots.

"Verl?" she called softly.

"I 'lows I'll 'ave to go feed those dogs," answered Verl as he put on his jacket and started for the stairs.

"Be careful," warned Sharna. "They may snap you. I 'lows they're awful 'ungry. They've been 'owling nearly all night."

"If they snap at me," said Verl, "I'll 'it 'em!" and he went down the stairs.

It was not strange that Verl left off the letter "h" from some of his words, for in Rocky Bay almost everybody talked that way. It was not unusual for an "h" to be put on where it did not belong, or left off where it was needed. What if they did mutilate the king's English a little? They understood one another. Of course the radio was having a good influence on those who wished to improve their speech. Also the folks who took trips and spent the winter "outside" were inclined to speak more properly than those who stayed in the village.

Sharna listened as Verl greeted mother in the kitchen. Then she heard him go out to the shed behind the house where were kept the chunks of seal meat and fish scraps for the dogs. She could hear him whistling one of his favorite cowboy songs as he went to the kennels. How the dogs barked and leaped and pulled against their chains when Verl came toward them. They were unruly and a bit vicious, for they were kept for the purpose of drawing sleds and komatiks (heavier sleds, or sledges) over the snow in the winter. It took a lot of food to keep them fed all summer. Their main food consisted of fish heads and scraps, with cooked corn meal of a coarse quality.

Sharna could tell by the different sounds when each dog received his portion of breakfast. She hoped the dogs would not snap at Verl. He knew how to manage them, and he always carried a stout stick when he went to care for them.

"Sharna!" called mother up the stairway.

"Yes, mother," answered Sharna.

"'Urry down now. Lots to do today. Ken! Don! Poggy!" she called to the boys. "Time to get 'round now."

There was a groan from the boys' room. Then came muffled sounds and a squeal or two as Ken good-naturedly pulled the covers off Don and Poggy. Next there was a scramble to get into clothes.

Sharna also wiggled into her blouse, slacks, and shoes, and reached the head of the stairs ahead of her brothers.

Down the stairs they went to take their turn at the wash pan and family towel. Then they sat down at their usual places at the table for breakfast.

They were all busily eating when Verl came in. It seemed to Sharna that he spent more time than usual at the wash pan. He even dipped up a second pan of water to wash. When he came into the kitchen he was wrapping a strip of cloth around his hand.

"Verl, you're 'urt?" inquired mother.

"Yes, old Smut was loose again. Been fightin'. 'E bit me when I snapped his chain."

"Better get rid of 'im," said Don. "Ya can't trust 'im. 'E's like his father, the wolf. 'E's vicious."

"But 'e's the best lead dog we 'ave," declared Verl loyally. "We'll keep old Smut, even if 'e is part wolf."

Mother looked across the table at Verl and said, "After you eat, you go right to the nursing station and get Miss Arletta to fix that 'and."

"But it's just a scratch," said Verl with a careless toss of his head.

"Verl!" When mother said his name that way, he knew she was in earnest. "I know you are 'most a man, son, but even *men* 'ave to get their dog bites fixed."

"I'll go," said Verl. He never argued with mother. After he had finished his breakfast he went up over the steep hill to the nursing station to have the gash on his hand dressed by Miss Arletta, the nurse in charge. Dog bites could be serious if they were not cared for right away. The nearest hospital was at Crystal Acres, sixty miles away.

Verl was fascinated by the ease and efficiency of the nurse as she cleansed and dressed the wound on his hand. She seemed so confident and sure.

"You really know 'ow to do it right," said Verl.

Miss Arletta smiled as she said, "That is one of the things they taught when I took my training in the big hospital at Crystal Acres. There you are, Verl. Maybe you had better let me dress it again for you tomorrow."

"It'll be all right now," said Verl. "Thank you, Miss Arletta." Soon Verl went back over the rocky path toward home.

When Sharna had finished her breakfast she began piling up the dirty dishes as her brothers left the table. She set out a clean bowl for Lolo, who had just come down the stairs and was washing her face. Mother was busy gathering up the laundry, for it was wash day. Soon there was a big pile of soiled garments, towels, checkered shirts, blouses, and blue overalls on the kitchen floor beside the big washtub. Mother was particular about her family; they must be in good health, well fed, and clean.

To wash clothes in the big tub was hard work. But that was the way it had been done in the village of Rocky Bay for many years. Electricity for lights or power machines was as yet unknown here.

Across the Cove

SHARNA," said mother, "as soon as you and Lolo get the dishes done you may go for red berries. Ken, Don, and Poggy are going for rabbits 'cross the cove."

"Is Verl going, too?" asked Sharna.

"No," said mother. "I 'lows 'e 'as a big pile of wood to cut."

" 'Ow many berries shall we get?" asked Lolo.

"Two pails full," answered mother. "I will make a pie tomorrow, and we will can some. 'Urry now. I will pack your lunch."

Sharna and Lolo hurried to finish the dishes. They were going to have fun picking berries while the boys snared rabbits. Soon they were on their way, swinging their empty berry pails and the lunch bucket as they went down the path and over the rocks to the landwash where the boats were kept.

Ken set the oar pins in the little holes provided for them and pushed away from the shore. The water was a bit rough in the cove, but Ken was a good rower, and he knew how to manage the boat very well. All the boys in Rocky Bay knew how to row boats. Each summer they went everywhere in their small homemade boats. Some of the older boys had outboard motors for theirs, but Ken, Don, and Poggy were satisfied to use oars.

Sharna and Lolo sat in one end of the boat holding the lunch and the empty pails. They pulled their head scarves tightly down over their ears, for the wind was cold as it blew across the cove.

Gusty gales in the springtime melted the snow and caused big waves in the bay to break the ice and pile it up in the landwash. There were cool breezes in summer that rustled the tiny flowers growing among the rocks. There were crisp autumn winds that brought the rains and filled the sails on the fishing boats as they went out into the deep sea for a haul. In winter came the cold, biting north winds that brought the blizzards and whirled the snow into big drifts. These were sharp, piercing winds that froze the ice in the little coves around Rocky Bay. Yes, the wind was always blowing, blowing, blowing!

Ken rowed hard against the wind. When the little boat reached the opposite shore, Don jumped onto the rocks and helped pull the boat up by a strong rope; then he and Poggy helped the girls climb out while Ken fastened the boat to a large stake farther up on shore. They all climbed up the rocky cliff above, where the wild birds nested in the springtime, where the frightened little rabbits scurried to hide under the low bushes, and where the red berries grew.

Sharna and Lolo busied themselves picking the red berries from the low bushes that grew in the marshy soil between the rocks. They did not mind the hard work, for they thought of the luscious pies and preserves that mother would make with the berries. The ones she would can in glass jars would be kept in the cellar along with the fruits and vegetables that were brought in on the big steamer from markets far to the south. The supplies of fruit, vegetables, eggs, canned milk, and meat came twice a month.

The sun climbed high and was starting to go down toward the western horizon. Sharna placed another handful of berries in her pail and then called to Lolo, "My pail is full now. Let's go down to the boat and eat our lunch. I'm getting 'ungry."

"Me, too," said Lolo. She followed Sharna over the rocks and across marshy places to the cliffs that bordered the water's edge where the boat was tied. Don was waiting in the boat. He had already eaten his share of the lunch, and was admiring the wild duck he had caught.

"We got our pails full of red berries," said Lolo proudly. "Aren't they pretty?"

"M-m-m. They look good," said Don.

"Where are Ken and Poggy?" asked Sharna.

"I 'lows they'll be coming soon," said Don. "They must be getting 'ungry, too." He gave three shrill whistles through his teeth, then paused to listen.

From somewhere above the cliffs, among the rocks there came an answer—two long whistles, then five short ones.

"They're coming," said Don.

The children had their own code for signaling to each other when they became separated or were in trouble. Verl, the oldest, signaled by one long whistle. Two whistles meant Ken, three meant Don, four meant Sharna, and five, Poggy. Lolo did not know how to whistle, but she could count, so she blew six short blasts on the little whistle that hung from a string around her neck.

Soon Ken and Poggy made their appearance. Ken proudly held up a rabbit that he had snared.

"I had two of 'em," said Ken, "but one got away."

"What did you find, Poggy?" asked Sharna.

"I found something, but I don't know what 'e is," said Poggy. " 'E's too 'eavy to carry, so I tied 'im up with my rope; but I don't know what 'e is."

"Show us where you left 'im; we'll help you," offered Ken.

Ken, Don, and Poggy climbed back up the cliff and over the rocks to the place where Poggy had left his captive. Ken and Don were quite surprised to see what Poggy had tied up with his short piece of rope.

" 'Ow did you catch 'im?" asked Ken.

"I just came up behind 'im, slow and easy. 'E was lying down behind some bushes. I must 'ave scared 'im. 'E tried to get up, but 'e fell down again, so I quick tied up the 'ind legs; but I found 'e was too 'eavy for me to carry down to the boat. What is 'e?"

"Don't you know, Poggy?" asked Ken.

Poggy shook his head.

" 'E's a young deer," said Ken. " 'E must 'ave come down from the big woods beyond Wolf's Head. 'E's crippled—been shot in the leg. That's why 'e couldn't run." Ken stooped down to examine the injured front foot.

"A deer!" echoed Poggy, feeling quite proud of himself. "I didn't know I caught a deer!"

"Mother will really be surprised this time," said Don. "We'll 'elp you carry 'im down to the boat. 'E's a pretty little thing; wish we could keep 'im for a pet."

"But we can't keep *pets*," objected Ken, "because of the dogs. And we can't make pets of the dogs because they can't be trusted."

"But 'e's so pretty," said Don stroking the soft brown back of the trembling animal. He fastened the rope more securely around the back legs, and tied the front ones with his snare rope that he always carried in the back pocket of his jeans.

The boys carried the creature down to the boat.

"Careful now," cautioned Ken. " 'Old the boat steady, Sharna."

They had a bit of trouble, for the deer struggled and strained, but finally they managed to get it into the boat.

"I'll row back," said Don to Ken. "You rowed over here."

Lolo sat shivering in the end of the boat, holding tight to Sharna's hand.

" 'E won't 'urt you, Lolo," Sharna reassured her. " 'E's tied; and, anyway, a deer won't bite. 'E's afraid of us, that's why 'e wiggles. 'E wants to go back to the big woods to be with 'is mother."

"I 'lows it's a good thing you found 'im, Poggy," said Ken. "If 'e 'ad stayed there, the wolves would 'ave got 'im, sure. Is there any lunch left in the bucket? I'm 'ungry."

"So'm I," said Poggy.

Sharna handed the lunch pail to Ken. "We 'ad ours, so you and Poggy can 'ave what is left."

Sharna tied Lolo's scarf tighter around her ears. The wind was still blowing, and the waves splashed against the sides of the boat.

The deer struggled and kicked, trying to be free.

"Isn't 'e pretty?" said Don. "But I 'lows my duck is pretty, too."

"So is my rabbit," said Ken between bites of sandwich. "All wild things are pretty."

Lolo looked down at the pail of red berries by her feet.

"Our red berries are pretty, too," said Lolo.

When the children reached home, Ken fastened the boat firmly to one of the stakes along the shore of the landwash. Then he helped Don carry the deer up over the rocks toward home. Sharna, Poggy, and Lolo followed, bringing the rabbit, the wild duck, and the pails of red berries.

"I can carry the empty lunch pail," said Lolo. "It isn't 'eavy now."

When the children reached the house they proudly showed mother their treasures, the trophies they had found and brought home from across the cove.

"I 'lows you 'ad a good day," said mother. "Maybe Verl can get Tommy and his father to 'elp you take care of the deer. But, now, Ken and Don, go to the spring for some fresh water. Supper will soon be ready."

The Big Question

THE children ate a hearty supper, and after the dishes were washed, Sharna and Lolo sat on their stools near the battery radio, listening to the music. The boys were out behind the dog kennels with some of the neighbors.

Soon Don came in and stretched himself out on one of the little rugs on the floor.

"Sharna," said mother, standing in the doorway, "there are clothes to be folded while you listen. Lolo can fold the washcloths. Then you put 'em away where they belong."

"All right, mother," said Sharna, bringing the basket back to where she had been sitting on the low stool. She did not mind folding clothes. They smelled fresh and clean after blowing in the brisk wind.

"I wish father were home," said Lolo. "When will 'e come?"

"In November," said Sharna. "It will be cold then. Snow will be on the ground."

"Is it far to White Lake where the iron mines are?" asked Lolo.

"I 'lows it's an 'undred miles," said Sharna, giving the pile of towels another pat.

"Will Verl go back to the mines with father in the spring?" asked Lolo.

"Maybe. 'E will be old enough by that time," said Sharna.

Lolo was silent for a moment, then she asked, "Who will take care of the dogs while 'e is gone?"

Don looked up and said, "Lolo, why don't you keep still for a minute, you little question box? It's time for our story to begin."

Sharna and Lolo silently folded the clothes and stacked them neatly away where they belonged. They returned to the room and sat on their stools to listen to the radio. The other boys came in, washed their hands at the wash bench, and stretched out on the floor beside Don. Mother lighted the oil lamp and sat down in the easy chair with her mending.

All too soon the story ended. Mother laid aside her mending and announced, "Bedtime now. You've been away all day and need your rest. Busy day again tomorrow, canning red berries and straightening up the ice 'ouse. Don't forget to say your prayers."

A bit reluctantly, Ken rose from his position on the floor, snapped off the radio, and took off his heavy boots. As Verl arose from his favorite rug, he said, "I 'lows I'd better go check the dogs. I'll be back in a little while."

Sharna and Lolo made the necessary preparations for the night. They knelt beside the bed and repeated the words of the prayer they had been taught. When Lolo

had crawled in between the covers, Sharna blew out the
kerosene lamp and crawled into bed.

"Sharna," began Lolo, "why do we say prayers?"

"I—I don't know," admitted Sharna, a bit surprised
at the question.

Sharna had always taken it for granted that prayers
must be said. She could not explain why, except that
it was a daily duty, a perfunctory sort of ritual in which,
for her, there was no meaning. Lolo continued to ask,
"Who is 'our holy omnipotent Father'? Does He work
in the iron mines at White Lake, too?"

"I really don't know," said Sharna. "You *are* a little
question box tonight, aren't you?"

"But I really want to know," said Lolo. "I learn
about God in church, of course. I guess He must be
somebody special, like a movie star."

"Well, maybe—" Sharna shrugged her shoulders and
settled her head in the soft pillow to think. She had
never really given any thought to that question. Perhaps
LuDell, her friend who lived along the cove on the other
side of Lookout Rock, might know. She was a bright
girl, quite advanced for her age. Sharna would ask
LuDell in the morning, "Who is 'our holy omnipotent
Father'?" Yes, that was a question that was too big for
Sharna to answer.

On the Lookout Rock

LOOKOUT ROCK was a special meeting place for Sharna and her friend LuDell. It was a high rock between their homes, near the cliff that hung out over the water of the cove.

As soon as her morning work was done, Sharna tied her scarf over her short curly brown hair and scrambled up on Lookout Rock to wait for LuDell. From the smooth wind-swept surface of the rock, Sharna could see far out over the sparkling water that widens into the bay and on toward the distant horizon. Somewhere beyond that faint gray line to the south was Canada, where Eaton's mail-order house was. It was from Eaton's big catalogue that they ordered their clothing and supplies, which came on the big steamer in the summertime.

Far to the east was the Atlantic Ocean. Sharna had never seen the ocean—she had not even been as far east as Crystal Acres, sixty miles away, where the hospital was located. But mother had told her about the ocean. It was much, much bigger than the bay. It was big and blue and very deep. Sometimes huge icebergs floated in the water.

Far to the north was the North Pole. The Eskimos lived in the northland in crude little houses. Sharna did not know much about the Eskimos, except that their skin was dark and that they also traveled by boat and dog teams. It was in the Far North that the great white polar bears lived. They slept in caves of ice and went swimming and fishing in the icy water.

Far to the west at White Lake were the iron mines, where father worked from early March until November. Also to the west, beyond Wolf's Head, were the forests of spruce, hemlock, and birch that furnished the wood for building houses and boats. The men and boys went many miles inland to get wood for fuel. They had shacks in the forests where they camped at night. In the daytime they chopped the wood, stacked it, and carried it home on boats or komatiks. It would soon be time for Verl to go with the older boys to cut wood.

It was a big world outside, but the people of Rocky Bay were satisfied to stay in their little village and hunt and fish. Their fruit, vegetables, and supplies were brought in by boat; they had plenty of fish and wild game, berries and sea food. There was plenty for all. They would stay home with family and friends and be content.

"Sharna," called LuDell as she hurried up the path toward Lookout Rock.

As soon as the two girls were seated on the rock, LuDell began, a bit breathlessly, "Sharna—she's coming!"

"Who's coming?"

"The teacher. Soon as the teacher from 'outside'

comes in on the boat, we're going to 'ave school."

"School?" echoed Sharna. She did not know whether to be happy or sad. She listened carefully as LuDell told her of the letter grandfather had received from the teacher.

"Well," said LuDell, "don't just sit there, solemn as an owl; say something!"

"I know school will be all right," began Sharna, "but a teacher from 'outside'! She will wear fancy clothes and laugh at the way we talk. I wish my Aunt Minnie could teach us again. She was a good teacher. We don't really want a teacher from 'outside.' "

"Sharna," said LuDell, "you are not 'appy about school?"

"No," admitted Sharna, "but I 'lows we'll just 'ave to go." Then after a few moments she added, "I want to learn, though."

The two girls were both "solemn as owls" as they sat on the rock. Each was thinking about the new teacher that was coming from the modern world; from the world that scorned the simple mode of living of the little village of Rocky Bay, where all was peace and contentment in the homes of the humble fishermen.

No doubt tomorrow all the mothers in the village would take buckets of water, soap, and cleaning cloths and scrub the little schoolhouse from ceiling to door-step. The fathers would nail down the shingles, seal the windows against the cold and wind, to make the building snowproof. They would also put up new stove-pipes for the heater. Soon the big boys in the village would go away to the forest to cut fuel. Of course Verl would miss several days of school, but that did not matter.

Soon Verl would be a man and go to work in the iron mines with father. He would not need an education to do that. And if he did not get a job in the mines he could always get out his cod nets and go fishing.

"Well," said LuDell, "if I 'ave to go to school, I 'ave to. But I am going to get a new permanent before school starts. My new clothes we ordered from Eaton's should be on the next boat."

"LuDell," said Sharna, "I 'ave an idea. Let's be really good in school this year, and show that teacher from 'outside' that she isn't the only smart one. I will work 'ard. 'Ow about you?"

LuDell was doing some serious thinking. Suddenly she gripped Sharna's hand. "Let's do it! We'll show 'er we're not dumb."

"It will be our secret," said Sharna. "We will not tell anyone, not even our mothers or fathers."

"Not even 'our holy omnipotent Father,'" said LuDell, solemnly.

"I was going to ask you," began Sharna hesitantly, "who is our holy omnipotent Father? Lolo was asking me last night when we said our prayers."

"Why, Sharna!" said LuDell in a shocked tone. "Don't you know?"

"Yes, but I just didn't know 'ow to explain it to Lolo. You tell me."

"Well," began LuDell, trying for the first time to really think something out for herself, "our holy ominpotent Father is the big God who lives up by the North Pole. He is very strong. He makes the wind blow, and He makes the ice freeze in the coves. He sends down the snow and blizzards in the winter. Sometimes He makes great fire come out of His throne to devour the wicked people. The fire comes right out of the sky. He even takes away your breath when you die!"

" 'Ow do you know?" asked Sharna.

"Oh, I just listen in church," said LuDell with a knowing toss of her head.

"Do you know what 'omnipotent' means?" asked Sharna, after a brief silence.

"I 'lows that means a great king, one who is cruel and terrible. I'm glad I don't live up by the North Pole, aren't you?" asked LuDell, shaking her head solemnly.

"But," objected Sharna, "if God is holy, 'ow could He be cruel and terrible?"

"I really don't know," admitted LuDell.

"Well, we could go and ask Aunt Minnie," suggested Sharna. "She was our teacher last year, and she finished the seventh grade."

"Or we can wait and ask the new teacher," said LuDell. "She should know *everything*. She's from 'outside,' where folks get educated. Grandfather said the new teacher has a college degree, and that is even better than seventh grade, I guess. That's even better than your Aunt Minnie."

"LuDell," chided Sharna, "you know very well that Aunt Minnie would still be our teacher, except for Uncle Joe."

"Yes, I 'lows she would. I'm sorry, Sharna; I like your Aunt Minnie, too. Please tell me again about your Uncle Joe."

When Uncle Joe Was Lost

SHARNA liked to tell stories, and she enjoyed listening when a story was being told. As she listened she tried to picture in her mind the people, the places, and the things the story was about.

As book learning in Rocky Bay was limited, the people acquired much of their knowledge through the stories that were told. Even the smaller children could repeat a story in minute detail, and they absorbed all the neighborhood gossip they could pick up while listening to the older folks talk.

Sharna was a good storyteller, and she had often entertained Lolo and the boys for hours at a time. But since the radio came, they all enjoyed the stories that came from the little box. These stories, especially some of them, were different, new, and exciting.

Sharna shifted her position on the big rock in order to look far out over the cove. She loved her Uncle Joe and never tired of telling the story of how he became a cripple.

"It 'appened one night in the winter," began Sharna.

"It was bitter cold, and the bay was frozen over, so the boats could not bring the mail. Uncle Joe took 'is komatik and dog team and went up to Echo Point, eight miles from 'ere, to bring the mail from the airport. It was nice when 'e left 'ome. The sun was shining, and the wind was not blowing too 'ard. But before 'e left Echo Point, it got cold; it began to snow, and the wind blew terrible.

"Uncle Joe was dressed warm, with 'is 'eavy coat and parka, big thick mittens and overshoes. 'E even 'ad a thick scarf to tie around 'is neck.

"Well, the wind kept blowing, and the snow whirled around in 'is eyes, so 'e could 'ardly see where 'e was going. 'E wandered around for hours and hours, but 'e couldn't find the cliff trail. 'E thought 'e was lost for sure. It was beginning to get dark, too, and Uncle Joe 'ad all the mail on 'is komatik. I 'lows 'e was really worried about that mail. 'E was afraid, too, that 'ungry timber wolves might find 'is trail and follow 'im."

Sharna hesitated. She was picturing the scene in her mind, trying to imagine every vivid detail.

"It was so cold," continued Sharna, "that Uncle Joe thought 'e was going to freeze. 'E tried to walk behind the komatik, but 'is feet were too numb. So 'e just kept riding, trying to find the cliff trail; but the wind was blowing so strong 'e could 'ardly breathe. 'E wandered around for hours and hours, and then 'e finally gave up trying. 'Is 'ands were so cold 'e couldn't 'old on any longer, so 'e stopped the dogs and shifted the mail bags so 'e could lie down on the komatik. 'E covered up with the 'eavy robe and went to sleep. But the dogs just kept on going. They wanted to get 'ome out of the storm. 'Ow they found the cliff trail, Uncle Joe did not know. But if they 'ad not kept going, poor Uncle Joe would 'ave frozen to death.

"It was about four o'clock in the morning when Aunt Minnie 'eard the dogs barking and knew 'e 'ad come 'ome. Uncle Rex came and 'elped 'er get 'im in bed, and 'e stayed there for many weeks. Even the doctor from Crystal Acres came to take care of 'is feet; they were both frozen.

"So, that is why 'e sits in 'is wheel chair and Aunt Minnie takes care of the post office. 'E can't even go fishing any more." To the people of Rocky Bay, the inability to go fishing was almost a tragedy, for to gather in the scaly spoils of the sea was their life.

LuDell was well acquainted with the situation. Many times she had seen Uncle Joe sitting helplessly in his wheel chair by the window, while Aunt Minnie was busy doing the work in the little post office and what other work she could find to do.

She was the village beauty operator and earned a bit of extra money giving permanent waves to the women and girls.

"I like your Aunt Minnie," said LuDell. "She is a good teacher. I want to see if she will give me a permanent tomorrow if she is not too busy. I want to look nice when school begins."

"Let's go down to the post office right now," suggested Sharna. "If she is not too busy, we might even ask 'er about the holy omnipotent Father. She should know; she plays the organ in church."

Uncle Joe was sitting in his usual place by the window in his wheel chair, sorting out the mail on the table before him. He greeted the girls as they came in the door.

"Good morning, Uncle Joe," said Sharna. "Where's Aunt Minnie?"

"I'm back here, Sharna," called Aunt Minnie from the living quarters in the rear of the building. "As soon as I dry my hands I'll be right out."

"Word comes that you girls are going to 'ave a new schoolteacher," said Uncle Joe, leaning back in his chair.

The girls nodded.

"And I understand she is going to stay with your grandfolks, LuDell."

"Yes," said LuDell.

"It will be good for the old folks to 'ave company this winter. Seems they don't get out so much any more."

"Oh," said LuDell, "grandmother can still keep 'ouse, and grandfather can fish."

As soon as LuDell finished her sentence she was sorry she had spoken. She saw the strange look that came over Uncle Joe's face. The girl glanced down at his crippled feet. She was glad that Aunt Minnie came into the room just then to make arrangements for the permanent wave.

For several minutes they visited with Aunt Minnie. Then Sharna asked, "Aunt Minnie, can you tell us who our holy omnipotent Father is? And what does 'omnipotent' mean?"

"Well, that is a big order, Sharna. I've never really given it serious thought. I guess I have always taken it for granted and let the preacher explain it to us in his sermons. If I were you, I wouldn't worry your pretty little heads about such questions. Just go to church, say your prayers, and be good girls. Then when you get old enough you can join the church and take Communion."

Aunt Minnie patted Sharna on the arm, and the girls prepared to leave.

"Is your father fishing today?" Uncle Joe asked LuDell.

"No," said LuDell; " 'e's gone for mackerel. Grandfather went with 'im, I think."

The girls said Good-by to Uncle Joe and Aunt Minnie and wended their way over the rocks toward home. LuDell was happy about the permanent wave she would have the next day, but Sharna was a bit disappointed because Aunt Minnie could not give her a satisfactory answer to her question.

"LuDell," said Sharna, as they parted near Lookout Rock, "I 'lows we'll just 'ave to wait till the new teacher comes to find out about the holy omnipotent Father."

"Yes," agreed LuDell, "we'll 'ave to wait."

The Teacher Arrives

IT WAS an exciting day for the people of Rocky Bay. Nearly everyone in the village was down at the wharf when the supply steamer docked. Ken, Don, and Poggy were thinking of the new checkered shirts, blue overalls, warm zippered jackets, and high laced boots that would be theirs when they received their packages from Eaton's mail-order house.

"And my new cowboy suit," said Poggy. "It will 'ave a leather belt with a steer-'orn buckle."

"Mine will 'ave a steer-'orn buckle, too," said Don.

Sharna, LuDell, and Lolo walked hand in hand to the wharf. They were anxious to see the new teacher from "outside."

"I wonder what she will be like," said LuDell.

"I am all shaky inside," said Sharna. "And my 'eart is beating so fast."

"I 'ope we don't miss 'er in all this crowd," said LuDell, peering around the bystanders.

"Maybe that is our teacher," said Sharna, indicating one of the incoming passengers.

"No," decided LuDell, "she dresses the same as we do. Teacher will be different, coming from 'outside.' "

The girls waited and waited. The men were busy unloading the cargo. Several persons were hurrying to and fro, talking excitedly. Boxes and barrels and bundles were piled up on the wharf. Crates of fruit and vegetables were unloaded and were distributed according to previous orders. The mailbags were taken to the post office.

Sharna was becoming discouraged, and she said, "I've been looking and looking. Maybe she didn't come."

"She must 'ave come," said LuDell. "The letter to grandfather said she was coming on this boat."

"But there are so many people," said Lolo. "Perhaps we missed her."

Someone spoke to Sharna from the crowd. It was Verl. "Did you see 'er?" he asked.

"See who?" asked Sharna.

"The teacher," said Verl. "I helped take her trunks up to LuDell's grandfolks. She's up there now."

"Let's go," said LuDell, taking Lolo by the hand and making her way through the crowd.

It was not far over a little hill beyond the wharf to grandfather's house. As they neared the unpainted cottage on the rocks they saw grandfather bringing in an armload of wood. He welcomed the girls.

"Come in out of the wind," he called.

Sharna was a bit hesitant. She wanted to meet the new teacher; but, now that she was so near, the girl suddenly felt very shy.

"Come on," urged LuDell, and the girls followed grandfather into the house and stood near the door.

The girls waited for the new teacher, but no passengers appeared. Then Verl told the girls that the new teacher had gone to LuDell's grandfolks' house.

Grandmother was busy putting dishes on the table. The teakettle was singing merrily on the stove.

"We will soon 'ave something 'ot for the teacher to drink," said grandmother. "I 'lows she must be 'bout worn out after her long trip."

Grandmother smiled proudly as she introduced the girls. "This is your new teacher."

There was a friendly, winning smile on the kind face of the teacher. Her manner revealed the fact that she had come from the world beyond the horizon. Her voice was soft and sweet as she said, "I am very glad to meet you girls. I am sure we'll have many good times together this year. I know I am going to love every one of my pupils."

Somehow the new teacher seemed to be "one of us," as Sharna confided to the family that night at the supper table.

"You would never know she was from 'outside,'" said Sharna. "I know I am going to like school after all."

That evening the boys did not listen to the radio. They were so busy admiring their new clothes that they forgot to turn it on. Ken and Don tried on their new boots. Poggy was decked out in his cowboy suit and hat, the belt with the steer-horn buckle, and the gun holster.

"Poggy," said Don, "I'll trade you my new jackknife for your gun 'olster."

"No," said Poggy.

"I'll give you my slingshot and ten marbles to boot," offered Don, holding them out temptingly before him.

"No trade," said Poggy firmly. "This came with my cowboy suit, and I'm going to keep it."

"Shame on you, Don," chided Verl from the depths of his new warm zippered jacket.

"I was only teasing," said Don with a grin. "I didn't want 'is 'olster. I 'ave one of my own."

Ken was busy untying a knot in one of his boot strings. He addressed his older brother, Verl, by asking "What are you going to take to teacher on the first day of school?"

"Who, me?" Verl turned to Ken. He partly closed his eyes and doubled up his fists as if ready for a fight.

"Yes, you," said Ken. "I 'lows we always take something to the teacher."

There was a light scuffle between Verl and Ken. They enjoyed a good-natured tussle now and then.

"Now, don't you worry about what I'll give the teacher. I 'lows I'll 'ave something in a few days." Verl looked down at his brother sprawled on the floor.

When Verl came to Sade's kennel, she would not let him come near. She snarled and snapped viciously at the stick he carried. He could hear strange noises.

More Dogs

TWO busy days went by as the children prepared for school. On the second evening mother lighted the lamp and placed it on the table in the living room. Verl turned on the radio and stretched out on the floor beside Ken to enjoy a good story with the family. Don soon joined them. Sharna, Poggy, and Lolo were playing a game with marbles in one corner of the room.

"Only one story tonight," decided mother. "You 'ave to get a good night's sleep; tomorrow you are off to school."

"Yes, mother," said the children in chorus. They had long ago learned to obey their parents in all things. They never argued when mother spoke. She was the head of the family while father was away, and they never questioned her judgment.

When the radio program was finished, Verl snapped the little button and went to see that the dogs were securely fastened in their kennels for the night. As Verl went on his little tour of inspection, he spoke kindly to each dog while he checked all the chains and snaps.

"Down, Jip. Easy there, Blackie. Get back, Smut."

When he came to Sade's kennel, she would not let him come near. She snarled fiercely and snapped viciously at the stick he carried. Verl could hear strange sounds back in the darkness.

"M-m," he said to himself, "I 'lows she 'as puppies in there." He gave old Sade some food and then flashed his light in the back of the kennel.

As he returned to the house he whistled a merry tune. Old Sade was his dog; the puppies would be his also. He really did not need them all, for he already had a good dog team. Perhaps he could sell them when they grew big and strong.

The boys were in bed by the time Verl went upstairs.

"Guess what?" began Verl.

"Old Smut was loose again?" offered Ken.

"No."

"Cash and Jip been fighting?" asked Don.

"No, old Sade has her pups," stated Verl.

Ken sat up in bed. " 'Ow many?"

"Five."

Poggy and Don both sat up in bed. "What color?" asked Don.

"One all white, one all black, and three spotted like Sade."

"Wish I could see 'em tonight," sighed Poggy. But he knew mother would not permit him to get up once he was in bed.

"You can see 'em when I feed the dogs in the morning," said Verl. " 'Tain't safe to go near old Sade now. She's vicious."

The three boys settled back on the pillows, and soon Verl blew out the light.

"What are ya goin' to do with five more dogs?" asked Ken.

"Don't know yet," mused Verl; "but I 'lows I can sell three of 'em to a man over in Wolf's Head, beyond the wharf. I'll keep the black one. 'E'll be a good mate to Jip when 'e gets big."

"What about the other one? You said there are five." Poggy had been busy counting on his fingers. He wondered what would become of the fifth puppy.

"I 'lows I'll just give 'im to the teacher," said Verl.

Ken and Don laughed heartily.

"Well, that's just what I plan to do," said Verl definitely. "You'll see."

Verl curled up under the wool blankets. The subject was closed.

There were stifled giggles from Ken and Don. Then all was quiet in the upstairs room where the boys slept.

It was quiet also in the girls' room. Lolo was sound asleep; but Sharna was still awake, thinking about school and the new teacher.

"I know I'm going to like school," said Sharna to her pillow.

The First Day of School

LONG before the sun, like a golden ball, came up from behind the rugged cliffs, the children of Rocky Bay had been making preparations for school. Their faces were scrubbed and beaming; their hair was neatly combed; their new school clothes were buttoned and zipped; their lunches were packed and placed beside the tablets, crayons, and carefully sharpened pencils. Today was the first day of school!

From the scattered houses came the children, scrambling over the rocks and running on the paths on their way to the one-room schoolhouse. In addition to the regular school supplies and lunch pail or basket, each child carried some token to give to the new teacher. Some of the parents breathed a sigh of relief as they watched their little ones go—*not* that they placed much value on education, for many of the parents could neither read nor write; but they were glad to get them out from underfoot. Some of the parents did not care if their children were absent from school, for few of the villagers had gone beyond the seventh grade. The older children were not inspired to become teachers, doctors, or nurses, or to take a wider interest in the concerns of the world. Their only ambition was to remain in their own village and to fish.

Sharna and Lolo met LuDell on the rocky path. Verl raced with his brothers over the hill to the schoolhouse.

The teacher was busy putting pictures on the wall when the children entered. She turned to greet them as each child placed his or her gift on the desk.

"I brought a jar of red berries," said Sharna. "I helped mother can them."

"I helped pick 'em," added Lolo, shyly.

"They are lovely," said the teacher. "Thank you very much."

Ken placed a small red boat on the desk. "You can keep your pencils in it," he said. "I carved it by myself. I painted it, too."

"Thank you, Ken. It is very pretty," said the teacher.

"I brought you a wild-duck egg," said Don. "I found it across the cove. It's kinda old, so I wouldn't 'vise ya to eat it."

"Thank you, Don. I will try not to break it," said the teacher with an amused smile on her face. She put it in a safe place on her desk, where it would not roll off to the floor and break.

Poggy placed his gift on the desk. The teacher laid back the heavy wrapping paper and said, "Oh, thank you, Poggy. These are lovely fish."

Poggy looked at the teacher and said in a rather disgusted tone, "Them ain't *fish*; them's herring!"

Verl saw the puzzled expression on the teacher's face,

Poggy placed his gift on teacher's desk. When she opened the paper, Poggy held up a herring. "Oh, thank you, Poggy," she said. "These are lovely fish."

so he offered an explanation. "You see, teacher, up here when we say 'fish' we mean 'cod.' Them's just herring."

"I see," said the teacher. "Thank you, Verl. I'll try to remember." She gratefully acknowledged each gift in turn, knowing that in many cases, a real sacrifice was involved. They were bringing her their treasures because they looked up to her as someone special. To them she would be next to father or mother. When they called her "teacher" it was with an endearment almost akin to reverence. She would not insist that they call her by her name. "Teacher" would be sufficient, and with the help of the heavenly Father she would endeavor to be all that the title implied.

The gifts from the children were varied: a lump of coal, a strip of fur, a handful of marbles, a box of cookies, a well-worn slingshot, some fruit, and a partly chewed stick of gum, carefully replaced in its original bit of paper. The little donor could not refrain from tasting it before giving it to teacher, for gum was a rare treat in the village. There was also an assortment of cheaply bound books. On the crumpled paper covers were vivid Western scenes depicting cowboys, masked outlaws, and gunmen.

"Will ya read these to us, teacher?" asked Tommy, who was about the age of Verl.

The teacher hesitated before replying. This was not exactly the type of reading material she would choose to read before the class, and it was certainly not listed in the course of study. Glancing rapidly over a few of the pages, she found what she had expected. These stories were hardly worthy of the paper upon which they were printed. However, it was this type of "literature" the people of Rock Bay were familiar with, the kind they seemed to appreciate and enjoy. It was going to be rather difficult to introduce them to the standard classics and noted authors, and, above all, to the Book of books, the Holy Bible.

It was true, the people of Rocky Bay had Bibles in their homes. They went to church regularly and listened devoutly to a lot of monotonous repetitions. But they did not read the Scriptures in order to think for themselves; they did not know the love of God. To them the heavenly Father was a stern, cruel tyrant who ruled them with severity. They served Him through fear rather than because they loved Him.

"Will ya, teacher?" Tommy interrupted the woman's trend of thought by repeating his question.

"I will look them over and decide," she said as she smiled across the desk at Tommy. "I do appreciate your kindness in bringing them to school."

Verl stood awkwardly beside the desk. He seemed a bit embarrassed as he said, "I couldn't bring my gift to you this morning. But I 'lows I'll be bringing it one of these days. It's too little yet."

The teacher was curious and asked, "What do you plan to bring, Verl?"

"Well, the other night old Sade, that's one of my dogs, had five pups. I'll give you the little white one if you want it. He's a cute little one, and 'is mother is a good breed. I know you'll like the puppy when you see it."

Verl was so in earnest the teacher scarcely knew what to say.

"I appreciate your thoughtfulness, Verl, but where would I keep it?"

"Oh, I'll keep the puppy for ya, with 'is mother in the kennel, till 'e is big enough."

"That is very kind," said the teacher. "Thank you, Verl."

She watched the youth as he went across the room and sat down at one of the larger desks. Her heart went out to the older boys. They would soon be too big to come to school. They would be men and take their place with the fishermen or leave home to work in the iron mines. That would be the end of their education. How well these strong youth could fill the ever-growing need for doctors, missionaries, and teachers! How much good they could do in their own community with the education and training they might receive from the out-side world!

The teacher finished hanging the pictures on the wall. She looked at her watch; it was time to ring the bell to call the children to order.

"You may keep the desks you have selected, if you wish. Now who will choose a song to sing this morning?"

After several futile efforts to get the children to sing some of the old, familiar favorites, the teacher looked at the group of shy, giggling youngsters and asked, "Really, don't you like to sing together?"

Sharna was going to suggest that Verl could sing cowboy songs, but when she glanced in his direction she decided not to mention it. Instead she said, "We don't know 'ow to sing together. We just sing cowboy songs when we're alone."

Several of the children had become a bit hilarious at

the thought of singing, so the teacher decided to forget it for a few days. She endeavored to classify the children according to grade. She passed out textbooks and assigned lessons. By dinnertime she had partly won the confidence of the group who would be in her charge until spring. What a challenge they were! They must be taught to think for themselves, to read for information and pleasure, to have a curiosity about the outside world beyond their little world of fish.

When school was dismissed in the afternoon, Sharna, LuDell, and Lolo walked arm in arm toward home.

"I 'lows I am going to like school," said Sharna. "I'll study 'ard to pass my grade. I want to learn 'ow to read and write, and talk better, as she does. I like to 'ear 'er read to us. I can *see* the pictures of the things she reads about. I like the stories she reads to us from the Bible. They are even better than cowboy stories. Do you think we can memorize that psalm?"

"I am going to try 'ard," said LuDell.

"I learned some new words," said Lolo, "and I can write my name. I like to make little animals out of clay."

When Sharna and Lolo went to bed that night they said their prayers as usual.

Sharna lay under the blankets thinking, thinking. It had been a full day, with so many new and pleasant experiences. Most of all, the teacher had been kind to her. She had given her a new outlook on life.

"I wish someday I could be a teacher like 'er, even if she did come from 'outside,'" whispered Sharna.

The Church on the Hill

IT WAS a cool, crisp morning. The villagers of Rocky Bay wended their way up the hill to the little white church that shone in the sunlight. Sharna and Lolo walked up the steps behind Ken, Don, and Poggy. Verl and mother followed close behind.

"Remember, now," cautioned mother, "act like gentlemen and ladies in church. I don't want to be ashamed of ye."

All six children nodded their heads in assent. As far back as they could remember they had heard that admonition every time they walked up the steps of the church. Soft music came from the wheezy organ. Aunt Minnie was not the only one in the village who could play an instrument, but she had been elected church organist many years ago, and, because she was faithful to her weekly post of duty, no one thought of making a change.

Sharna was proud of her Aunt Minnie. She was kind and good, and she showed her love by the attention she gave Uncle Joe. Sharna looked around the room.

There was Uncle Joe, sitting at the rear of the church in his wheel chair. It was Uncle Joe's work to take care of the offering plates that were on the table beside him.

Sharna sat up straight and tall, looking toward the front. She saw the pulpit where the minister stood, the stained-glass window, and the candlesticks. Then she turned once to watch Aunt Minnie at the organ, solemnly following the notes in the songbook.

Sharna looked out of the corner of her eye to see the church members who were taking their seats in the congregation. There were Tommy and his parents, Bobby with his brothers and sisters. (His father also worked at the mines at White Lake.) Behind them sitting in their usual place were Uncle Tom and Auntie Lil, with Uncle Rex and Aunt Carol and their five little ones. There was something pathetic about Uncle Tom and Auntie Lil. Ever since their only daughter, Eulene, had gone "outside," they had become despondent. They seemed to have lost interest in life. Uncle Tom went fishing, of course, and Auntie Lil kept house; but as the days went by, the house showed signs of neglect. Then, too, the couple lost interest in their personal appearance and looked somewhat shabby.

On the other side of the room, near a window, sat Miss Arletta, who had charge of the first-aid and nursing station. She was always neatly dressed, though her clothes seemed plain and simple. She was friendly and had a smile for everyone. Sharna had often wished that someday she could be a nurse like Miss Arletta. But there would be much to learn, and she would have to go to the hospital at Crystal Acres for training. She might even have to go "outside" to complete her education.

"I guess I just won't be a nurse after all," said Sharna to herself.

Most of the families in the village were related in some way. Aunt Minnie was mother's sister. She was also a cousin to LuDell's mother, and sister-in-law to Uncle Rex.

LuDell's grandparents came in and sat down in their pew. The teacher was with them, dressed in a modest blue suit and tiny hat to match. Somehow, Sharna had expected the teacher to come to church dressed in fancy clothes, since she came from "outside." Certainly no one could find occasion to criticize the simplicity of her attire.

LuDell and her parents came down the aisle and slipped quietly into their seat. Aunt Minnie began playing the organ voluntary, and the members of the choir came in from the side room and took their places in the choir loft. The minister, dressed in his dark vestment, stood behind the pulpit.

Sharna had been a regular attendant at church since she could remember. It was all familiar to her: the songs by the choir, the reading of Scripture from the big book, the long sermon filled with big words, of whose meaning Sharna had not the slightest idea. But it was all a part of the ritual, the only form of divine worship she knew. Perhaps someday she would learn what the mysterious words meant.

Sharna had been taught to sit quietly and watch the minister while he was speaking. Above all, she must never talk or whisper during the Communion service, which was a sacred occasion.

Before the service was over, Sharna began to grow

restless. She glanced at teacher, who was listening intently to the minister's words. Sharna would ask teacher about some of those words, since she was to be a guest for dinner! There would be potatoes, stuffed partridge, red-berry pie, and other good things to eat. Sharna suddenly felt hungry just thinking about food. Mother had the food ready to put in the oven when they arrived home from church. Mother always planned her work well.

Sharna was so busy thinking of the visit they would have with teacher, she was surprised when Aunt Minnie began playing the closing hymn. It was time to go home!

Sharna stood with bowed head as the minister offered the benediction. As Aunt Minnie began playing again, the people left the church and went down the various paths to their homes.

"I'll race you home," said Ken.

"I 'lows I'll beat," said Verl, dashing on ahead of his three brothers. Poggy ran a few steps, then stopped to wait for mother and the girls. He knew he could not compete with those good runners. However, the boys did not go home. Instead, they ran down to the land-wash to see if any ice had formed in the coves.

The Missing Dinner

SHARNA opened the door so that her mother and the younger children might enter. Mother removed her wraps and put on her apron, ready to cook the dinner. As she was tying her apron strings she stood rather dazed before the table. There was no food in sight! The bread was gone, the stuffed partridge was gone, the red-berry pie was gone! The milk pitcher was standing empty, with a black rim around the top. The dishes showed a dark, smeary appearance. The covering cloth was on the floor, wrinkled and soiled. Mother looked around the room.

"Sharna! Whatever 'appened to the food?" asked mother in bewilderment.

Sharna came running into the kitchen with Poggy and Lolo at her heels. She also stared at the empty table.

"I 'lows it's gone!" she said, puzzling over the disappearance of the delicious dinner she had hoped to share.

Suddenly they heard a sound of scuffling upstairs. Mother went up to see what was going on, and she found eight dogs in the boys' bedroom tearing up a feather pillow.

With a few sharp words, mother ordered the dogs, "Git out of 'ere! Git!"

Down the stairs like a thundering herd went the somewhat surprised dogs. Sharna, Poggy, and Lolo stood huddled in a corner, fearfully watching as the animals raced across the living-room floor and out through an open window. They fell over one another in their haste to get out.

Mother followed them down the stairs and leaned against the wall. A wave of fear came over her as she realized she had dared to order eight vicious dogs out of her house. What if they had turned on her? She had no stick in her hand!

"Close the window, Sharna," said mother. "Poggy, go whistle for the boys. Verl will 'ave to learn to keep them chained!"

Mother cleaned up the dirty mess and scrubbed the table. Then she bustled around the kitchen putting things together to make an appetizing dinner. Soon the teacher arrived, and they visited merrily together. The boys came in and went upstairs to change their clothes.

"Mother," Don called down to her, "what 'appened to my pillow? Feathers are everywhere!"

Mother came to the foot of the stairs and explained.

"But I did check the dogs," said Verl. "I checked 'em before I went to church. They were all chained good. I can't understand 'ow they got loose. They just couldn't do it by themselves."

"I 'lows it was that gang of 'oodlums," said Ken. "They've been doing a lot of mischief all over the village."

Down the stairs like a thundering herd went the somewhat surprised dogs. Sharna, Poggy, and Lolo huddled in a corner, watching the vicious animals.

"Must be somebody unfastened them," said Verl.

"I saw 'em running around by the kennels, so I fed 'em and fastened their chains. Ken and Don 'elped me. I'll go out and check 'em again after I change my clothes."

The dinner was a success in spite of the change in the menu. While Sharna and Lolo washed the dishes, mother and the teacher sat in the front room and talked. Soon the girls joined them. Tenderly and tactfully the teacher asked questions. She did not ask to be curious or rudely inquisitive. Her only desire was to be friendly and kind and win the family's confidence.

During a slight pause in the conversation, Sharna said, "Teacher, I want to ask you a question I've been wondering about for a long time." The quaver in her voice showed her deep concern.

Laying a hand gently on her shoulder, the teacher asked, "What is it, Sharna?"

"I asked LuDell, but I don't think she really knows. Who is our holy omnipotent Father?"

For a moment the teacher hardly knew how to answer the girl. She knew the simple thinking of the people of Rocky Bay. They were all religious in a way and felt that church attendance and Communion were very important. But they did not know God as the loving Father of His children. How much depended on her answer!

"I'll gladly answer your question, Sharna," said teacher. "I think I shall start at the beginning and tell you a wonderful story. Would all of you like to bring up your stools and sit close beside me?"

Mother also listened as the teacher told the story of

the loving God who made a beautiful world for people to live in.

"He made the air that we breathe, the pure water that we drink, the fertile ground to raise the grain and vegetables that we use as food. He made the bays and streams to be the home of the fish and other sea creatures. He made the trees in the forest that we use for building material and fuel."

On through the story of creation she led them, constantly emphasizing the great love of the heavenly Father. The story of the Garden of Eden followed, with the temptation and sin of Adam and Eve. Then she explained why the Son of God made the sacrifice of His life for mankind.

"And someday," said the teacher, "that same Jesus is coming back to take us to heaven if we love Him and serve Him faithfully. I cannot tell you how beautiful heaven is, because nobody can even imagine how glorious and wonderful it will be."

"Will it be like the sunset we see from Lookout Rock?" asked Sharna. "Will it be all gold and shiny like the sun shining on the waves?"

"Perhaps that wonderful sunset is a little sample of what God wants to do for us because He loves us."

"Thank you, teacher," said Sharna when the story was ended.

"I hope I have answered your question," said the teacher.

"Yes," said Sharna simply. "I knew you could tell us about the holy omnipotent Father."

Long after the teacher had gone back to her boarding place, Sharna thought about the wonderful story. She tried to picture the beautiful angels that watch over the children of God. Would those angels take care of her father working in the iron mines? Perhaps it was angels that kept the dogs from snapping at mother when she drove them out of the upstairs bedroom.

"I want holy angels to take care of all of us," she said as she prayed that night. "Thank You for sending teacher to tell us about You."

The Fishing Boats Come In

IT WAS evening. Sharna and LuDell sat on Lookout Rock, talking over the events of the day. The girls had on warm jackets, and they wore scarves tied over their heads to keep out the wind that was colder than usual.

"I 'lows we'll 'ave winter soon," said LuDell. "The sun goes down in a different place. I like to see the pretty coloring on the bay when the sun sets."

"So do I," agreed Sharna. "It is beautiful. But I 'lows heaven will be even more beautiful. Teacher said so."

Sharna was silent for a few moments. Then she said, "LuDell, I found out who our holy omnipotent Father is. Teacher told me that He does not live at the North Pole or work in the iron mines. It is true He sends the snow in winter, and He makes the ice form in the coves. He loves us, and He even sends angels to take care of us. We can't see them, but they can see us. They keep us from danger lots of times. Teacher said the angels live in heaven. There are thousands and thousands of angels, and they all sing together. Maybe we should learn to sing together in school as teacher wants us to."

"I 'lows we could try," said LuDell.

"Teacher told me what 'omnipotent' means, too," continued Sharna.

"What does it mean?" asked LuDell.

"Teacher said it means 'unlimited power.' There is nothing too 'ard for God to do. He made the whole world because He loved us. He made the sun and the moon and the little stars we see in the sky at night. He made the oceans and the dry land. He even made this rock we are sitting on."

LuDell looked down and felt of the rock's smooth surface.

"I 'lows He made this just for us," said Sharna. "He made it because He loves us. He even sent His only Son to die for us."

LuDell looked out across the sparkling water at the sinking sun. "Really, Sharna?" she asked earnestly.

"Teacher said it is all in the Bible; so it must be true," said Sharna. "She is going to show me where to find it in the Bible, so I can read all about it when I learn to read better. She said I should learn to read for myself, and I'm going to try real hard."

The two girls sat on Lookout Rock gazing thoughtfully at the water. Suddenly Sharna pointed and said, "Look—over there. The fishing boats! They're coming in!"

"Where?" asked LuDell as she stood up.

"See those little black things—'way beyond Wolf's Head?"

The fishing boats docked at the fish stage, where the catch was cleaned, salted, and spread out on the rocks to dry. It was hard work, and everyone helped.

"Yes, I see them," said LuDell. "I 'lows they're the fishing boats, all right. Let's 'urry down to the village and tell everybody."

Away ran Sharna and LuDell to announce the arrival of the fishing boats. In a short time all the able-bodied men, women, and children of Rocky Bay were at the fish stage, ready to begin work as soon as the fish were unloaded from the boats.

It was hard work, for the fish must be cleaned, salted, and spread out on the rocks to dry as soon as possible. Everyone had to work fast. The fish stage was built on a platform extending out over the water like a tiny wharf, so that all the waste could be dumped into the water. It was early in the morning when the task was finished and the weary workers went slowly home to bed. They were tired, it was true, but they were used to hard work. Fishing was their lifework. Codfish was the main catch, but herring and mackerel were also caught in their season. Many families had their own trawler lines and spent much of their time fishing.

The next afternoon at sunset, Sharna saw LuDell waving excitedly to her from Lookout Rock. Sharna ran down the path and up over the rocks to meet her friend.

When Sharna reached the top of the rock she could only gasp, "I saw your signal."

"Guess what," began LuDell. "Eulene is back. She came in on the boat yesterday afternoon."

"Eulene?" echoed Sharna. "Back from 'outside'?"

"Yes. She's been away for about two years, working in a big factory in Canada. I guess she didn't like it in the big city, so she came back 'ome."

"I 'lows Uncle Tom and Auntie Lil are 'appy now," said Sharna.

"Oh, but Eulene isn't going to live with her folks. She's going to live with Uncle Rex and Auntie Carol and their five youngsters."

"But, why?" questioned Sharna.

"Eulene goes around with 'er nose in the air. She thinks she's too nice for 'er own folks any more, since she's been 'outside' and 'as nice clothes. She even thinks the 'ouse 'er folks live in isn't good enough."

"Is she glad to get back to Rocky Bay?" asked Sharna.

"Oh, yes, she told Tommy's mother that she didn't like domestic work, and the work in the factory nearly killed 'er. But she thinks she is smart. When she was at the fish stage last night she pretended she didn't know anything about fish. She looked at them and asked, 'Oh, are those little birds?' Then after a while she slipped on one and fell down. She jumped up and said, 'Oh, those dirty little herring!' She knowed *then* what they were!"

Sharna listened as LuDell repeated bits of village gossip.

"We really shouldn't talk about Eulene this way."

"That's right," said LuDell. "She is your cousin— and mine."

"I really feel sorry for 'er," continued Sharna. "I feel sorry for Uncle Tom and Auntie Lil, too. They 'ave been so sad and lonely. I 'lows they feel terrible that she doesn't want to live at 'ome. I'm sure Eulene is wrong about 'outside.' Teacher came from 'outside,' and she isn't proud. She even went to college! And Miss Arletta isn't stuck up, and she came from the big hospital in Crystal Acres. Someday I might go away to learn to be a nurse or a teacher. Maybe I'll be a missionary and tell the people about our holy omnipotent Father and 'ow He loves us. I might even go up north and 'elp the Eskimos."

"Sharna!" LuDell could hardly believe that she was hearing correctly. "Do you really mean it?"

"Yes," said Sharna solemnly. "When I get big I want to do something worth-while. I want to be like teacher. I want to do good as Jesus did."

It was LuDell's turn to be silent. She watched the golden setting sun sparkling on the waves as it played hide-and-seek behind the rose-colored clouds. The wind blew the curls from her serious face; there were miniature sunsets in her sparkling blue eyes.

"Now you are the one who is solemn as an owl," said Sharna.

"Well, I was thinking. I want to do something good, too; I want to be like teacher."

For several minutes both Sharna and LuDell watched the beauty of the scene below. Far over the water they could see the fishing boats going out for another haul. Somewhere down in the village, dogs were barking.

"LuDell," said Sharna breaking the spell, "sometimes I think God comes down to Lookout Rock. I can almost feel Him behind us. I want to be good; I want to go to heaven when Jesus comes."

"So do I" said LuDell. "Shall we go home now? It's getting cold, and I'm 'ungry. Your Uncle Joe said it's going to freeze tonight. 'E 'eard it on the radio."

"All right, let's go," said Sharna, starting down between the rocks.

The Night When the Sky
Was on Fire

GOING to freeze tonight," said Sharna to herself as she went down the path toward home. "Soon the bay will freeze over and the snow will come. Then we can walk across the ice when we go to school. We can take our sleds and slide down the big rocks. The boys will harness the dogs to komatiks, and we'll have lots of fun."

When Sharna opened the door, the appetizing odors of cooking greeted her.

"Just in time to set the table for supper, Sharna," said mother. "Lolo, get washed and call the boys."

After supper the children gathered with mother in the living room. The boys took their usual places on the floor to listen to the radio. They looked forward to evenings, when the best stories were broadcasted.

Poggy and Lolo played with tiny boats on the floor. Sharna held a skein of yarn while mother wound it into a ball. Then she watched as mother cast the stitches on her knitting needles. Sharna was anxious to see the new warm mittens finished, since they were for her. Mother always made the mittens for her children. They were stronger and warmer than the ones from the mail-order house.

Many of the mothers in the village of Rocky Bay spent the long winter evenings knitting for their children. Quite a number of the garments the children wore to school were homemade. Mother even made blue denim overalls for the boys. In the days gone by, grandmothers made many of the articles of clothing, the warm parkas, jackets, and sealskin boots. But nowadays most of the clothing, boots, coats, and parkas came from the big mail-order house in Toronto.

Sharna listened to the steady click, click of mother's knitting needles. She looked up into the tired face and saw the worry lines across mother's forehead. When father came home from the mines, mother would not have to work so hard.

Yes, Sharna was glad cold weather was coming. Father would soon be home, and the family would be united once more.

"Ah-o-o-o, ah-o-o-o." Somewhere in the village a dog howled. It was an eerie sound. The wind blew around the corner of the house, trying to get inside.

When the radio program was ended, Verl arose from his place on the fur rug to go out and check the dogs.

"I 'lows I'd better bring in some more wood so we can keep the fire going all night."

"Yes," agreed mother. "I 'lows it will freeze hard tonight—might even snow."

Verl put on his jacket and cap, took a lighted lantern and a stick, and went out the door. He had not been outside but a minute, when he came rushing in, calling, "Mother! Ken! Sharna! The sky is on fire! The sky is on fire!"

Mother and the children snatched their coats from the hooks by the door and hurried out.

"Look!" said Verl, pointing toward the north.

The whole sky seemed to be ablaze with shifting rows of light, tipped with dancing rainbow colors. Light streaks were leaping up from one circle to another, and the whole arch of fire seemed to be working upward toward the zenith.

Sharna clung to mother in fear. Could it be true what LuDell had told her? Could it be that the holy omnipotent Father lived up at the North Pole and was sending out fire from His throne to destroy the people? Was He cruel and terrible after all? The teacher had said He was good; but suppose the teacher was wrong. Sharna clung to mother in fear. From the region of the North Pole the glow seemed to spread out like a huge fan until the whole sky was a blaze of glory.

"Mother, what is it?" asked Sharna almost in a whisper. "Is it God coming down from the North Pole to destroy the wicked people? Are we so wicked that He will destroy us, too?"

"No, child, no. There is nothing to be afraid of. That is just the northern lights. Some people call it the aurora, but I 'lows it's the northern lights. It will fade out in a short while."

"Northern lights!" echoed Verl, Ken, and Don.

"I've seen it before," said Verl, "but I didn't know what it was. It sure is pretty."

"Northern lights!" exclaimed Sharna; "then the

teacher may be right after all." She looked up into the brilliant heavens with its ever-changing, ever-moving display of rainbow colors. It was even more beautiful than sunset from Lookout Rock.

"Isn't it pretty, Poggy?" said Lolo.

"Beautiful!" said Poggy. "Looks as if somebody is painting it."

"Somebody is," said Sharna; "just as He paints the sunsets. Our holy omnipotent Father is painting the sky with lights because He loves us. Teacher says He does many things for us."

"I wonder if father is looking at it over at White Lake?" questioned Verl.

"I 'lows 'e 'as been asleep for a long time," said mother. "Do you children realize it is almost midnight? We 'ave been standing out 'ere for quite a while, and it is cold. Into the 'ouse now, all of you. Time you were in bed."

"But the dogs, mother?" questioned Verl. "I 'ave not checked them yet."

"That's right, Verl. Go check your dogs." Taking Lolo by the hand, mother led the way back into the house to prepare for the night.

After making sure the dogs were secure, Verl brought in an extra armload of wood, banked the fire, and went upstairs to bed. Prayers were said, lights were blown out, and all was quiet.

"Thank You, dear God, for the beautiful northern lights," said Sharna, as she snuggled down beside Lolo under the warm covers. "Thank You for showing us 'ow much You love us. Amen."

And soon she, too, was fast asleep.

A Visitor in the Storm

FOR several days the cold wind blew down from the northeast. Ice formed along the edges of the landwash. Frost in the air seemed to bite and nip the rosy cheeks and noses of the children as they walked to the schoolhouse. Tiny flakes of snow, blown by the wind, felt sharp and prickly as they whirled into youthful faces.

"I don't like the snow," complained Lolo as she hurried along swinging her dinner pail. "It blows in my eyes."

Sharna pulled the scarf up over Lolo's face and took her mittened hand in hers. It was hard going against the wind. They met LuDell, also wearing a warm scarf over her nose.

"I 'lows winter is 'ere," said LuDell. "I 'ope the 'father of the week' made a good fire in the stove at the schoolhouse. When we get over the 'ill we can see if there's smoke." The "father of the week" was the parent who had his turn at caring for the schoolhouse. The families rotated this responsibility.

"I wish the wind wouldn't blow so 'ard," said Sharna, tucking her nose down into her warm scarf. "Mother 'lows father will be coming 'ome any day now; maybe today, if the boat comes in. But the waves are so 'igh, and it's so cold and stormy!"

" 'E'll be all right," LuDell assured her. "My father 'as gone seal hunting with a group of men. 'E left 'ome early this morning."

"I see smoke," said Sharna. "Tommy's father is 'father of the week.' 'E made a good fire in the stove to keep us warm."

When they reached the schoolhouse they took off their outer garments, hanging them neatly on nails near the door. They placed their dinner pails on the floor, and then they went to stand near the stove. There was something fascinating about the roaring and crackling of the burning wood.

Soon the little stove became a glowing red on one side, and teacher closed the draft. The little schoolroom was warm and cozy, a welcome spot for the children as they sought shelter from the storm.

Teacher was putting the best compositions on the bulletin board; but she paused to greet each child as he came in.

"I wonder if she put mine up," whispered Sharna to LuDell.

"Let's go and see," suggested LuDell.

"Yes, there's yours, and here is mine," said Sharna, proudly pointing to the neatly prepared lesson papers that were marked "Perfect."

The teacher smiled her approval. "You are doing well, Sharna," said the teacher. "I think you and

LuDell will be able to do the work of two grades this year. It will keep you busy, but it will be worth the effort. Would you like to try?"

"Oh, yes, teacher," said Sharna. "We'll work hard. We really want to learn; don't we, LuDell?"

"Yes," said LuDell. "Someday we each want to be a teacher like you."

"It will be a big undertaking," said the teacher, "but you are intelligent, and I am sure you can do the work of grades 3 and 4 this year."

The kind, understanding smile of teacher kindled a fire of love in Sharna's heart. It gave her the urge to do something great. It inspired her to study hard.

The children seemed restless during the morning session. Perhaps it was because the wind was blowing harder than usual. Sharna glanced out of the window now and then to watch the snowflakes blowing in their zigzag courses. Winter had come to Rocky Bay. She hoped that the boat bringing the men from the mines would be able to enter the harbor. She bent over her workbook again; there were many things to learn.

By dinnertime the storm had become severe. A real blizzard had struck Rocky Bay. Snow was piling up against the windows in the sixty-mile-an-hour gale; but inside the schoolhouse it was cozy and warm. Ken kept the fire going. He went again and again to the wood box for armloads of wood. Sometimes the fire became so hot in the stove that Sharna had to put her book in front of her face to protect it from the heat. It was a good feeling to have the security and warmth of the schoolroom when the storm was raging outside.

"I 'ope father isn't out in a boat in this blizzard!" she

said to herself. Then she suddenly remembered something. That very morning after teacher had rung the bell, she read some verses from the Bible about another boat in a stormy sea. Jesus had been in the boat with His disciples. The teacher had said that the holy omnipotent Father watches over the ships at sea. He takes care of His people in time of storm. Teacher had prayed for the safety of all who were out on the ocean in ships.

That gave Sharna an idea. She put her head down on her arms on the desk and prayed to the holy omnipotent Father. This time her prayer was not memorized words. She whispered to God as freely as she would talk to mother.

"Please take care of my father if 'e is out in a boat in this storm," she prayed, "because 'e is coming 'ome to us. 'E 'asn't been 'ome all summer. Please don't let 'im get cold in this blizzard."

Then she said "Amen," and raised her head. She was surprised to see teacher standing by her desk, looking down at her.

"Is there something troubling you, Sharna?" asked teacher kindly.

"There was, but it's all right now," said Sharna. "I was worried about my father out in this storm. Then I remembered what you read this morning, so I 'lowed I'd better pray about it. That's what I was doing. I'll get busy with my lessons right away," she added half apologetically.

Teacher patted Sharna gently on the shoulder and then turned away her face to hide a tear. Her mission in Rocky Bay was not in vain. The heavenly Father was no longer a tyrant to be dreaded and feared, for a trusting girl could go to Him with all of her problems.

"I'm glad that you've learned to call upon God in time of need," said teacher softly. "The Father loves you, Sharna, and is ready to answer your prayers. I'm sure He'll bring your father safely home from the mines. We will trust Him to do that, won't we?"

Sharna smiled and nodded. Then she bent over her book and soon had her papers ready to hand in.

The afternoon passed rather quickly. Poggy was coming down the aisle with the wastepaper basket. It was time to sing the good-night song and go home. The children did not feel embarrassed now when they tried singing together, for they had lost some of their shyness through games and rhythm exercises. Even Verl and Tommy joined in with their deeper tones. They enjoyed singing the familiar songs.

At the close of the song, when school was dismissed for the day, the door of the schoolroom suddenly opened. Someone came in, shaking the snow from his overcoat.

"Father!" said Don and Ken together.

"Father!" exclaimed Sharna, running to him. She put her arms around him, not heeding the cold, wet snowflakes that were still clinging to his coat.

He leaned down to embrace her.

"Oh, I knew God would bring you safe 'ome to us. I prayed to Him, and He did!"

Lolo and Poggy also came for their share in this happy greeting. Verl stood back a moment before coming forward to give his father a hearty handshake.

"I 'lows you 'ave been 'ome to see mother," began Verl.

"Yes, yes. She told me all of you were at school. So I decided to meet you here," said father.

Teacher cordially greeted Sharna's father, and then she helped the smaller children wrap up well before they went out into the storm.

Sharna hesitated a moment at the door. She wanted to say something to teacher, but did not know how to begin. The teacher noticed the brief pause and understood.

"Good night, Sharna," said teacher. "I know you are a happy girl."

"Good night," said the girl, with a smile.

The blowing snow whirled up into her face. She pulled her scarf over her nose so that only her eyes peeked out. She followed behind father, who was carrying Lolo and holding Poggy by the hand.

It was hard walking over the rocks and drifts of snow, but the group soon reached the warmth and comfort of home. Mother had a special supper cooking on the stove, in honor of father's return. Ken and Don brought in an extra supply of wood while Verl went out to care for the dogs. Poggy placed the overshoes on a rug by the door and swept up the wet snow that had scattered on the floor. Sharna and Lolo set the table and helped to serve the food.

A happy family gathered around the supper table that night in a wonderful reunion.

Verl Tries to Help

AFTER supper, mother lighted the big lamp and sat in her favorite chair, busy with her knitting needles. The children clustered around father to hear of his experiences at the mines. The boys stretched out on their favorite rugs. Sharna and Lolo drew their stools close to father's chair. Nobody even thought of turning on the radio, for the stories father told held their attention all evening.

Finally father said, "What is the weather forecast for tomorrow?"

As Verl snapped on the radio, lively orchestra music filled the room. Ken and Poggy tapped their feet, while Sharna and Lolo clapped their hands to the rhythm. Father seemed pleased.

"We learned to do it at school," said Sharna. "We even sing together now."

"I 'lows it's too early for the weather report," said Verl. "But we can listen to the music."

"Turn on a story," suggested Don.

"Too late," said Verl.

The music suddenly stopped. The radio announcer said, "We regret to interrupt this program, but we have a special news report. An airplane crashed a short time ago. The plane was en route from Crystal Acres to Echo Point, but because of the storm, it was forced down about two miles northeast of the village of Rocky Bay."

Father stood close to the radio to catch the details of the report. Then he said in sharp tones, "Verl, get your coat, robes, lanterns. I'll get out the big komatik and start harnessing the dogs."

"But—the storm!" objected mother.

"Not snowing now," said father, pulling on his heavy overshoes. "Snow's just drifting with the wind. We'll make it all right. Maybe we can 'elp the pilot. 'E may be 'urt bad."

In a short time, father and Verl were clad in warm coats, boots, parkas, and fur mittens. They harnessed the dogs to the big komatik and hung lighted lanterns on its sides to help guide them on the trail.

"Old Sade wants to go, too," said Verl; "but I told 'er to stay 'ome with 'er babies."

Old Sade barked and pulled at her chain as the dog team started down the hill with Smut in the lead. Jip, Cash, Blackie, Snap, and Boots leaped and bounded after him, barking and yelping excitedly. Away they went over the trackless snow toward the northeast. Father stood on the back of the komatik and called, "Ugh, ugh," which meant a right turn.

Verl pulled the heavy robe up around his neck, for the wind was cold and the dogs kicked the snow back into his face.

"Rada, rada," called father, a command for the dogs

to turn left. Smut had not forgotten his early training as a lead dog.

When two miles had been covered there was no sign of a plane anywhere. Verl thought he saw a dark object a little to the north, but when they reached the spot they found only bare rocks where the snow had been blown away.

"There it is!" called father, as a tiny light gleamed beyond the rocks. He directed the dogs toward the light and soon reached the wrecked plane.

Verl helped father lift the injured pilot out of the plane and onto the komatik. He was alive, but conscious only at intervals.

" 'E's 'urt bad," said father.

"Could we take 'im to Crystal Acres to the hospital?"

"Too far," said father. "We would never get 'im there in time."

"The nursing station at Rocky Bay?" asked Verl.

"We can try," said father.

The pilot roused himself and began reaching for something.

"My first-aid kit," he said huskily. "If I can only stop the bleeding. First-aid kit—" Then he lapsed into unconsciousness.

"I 'lows it's in the plane," said Verl, taking the lantern with him to see better. He found a box that he thought might be a first-aid kit, and brought it to father. Together they examined its contents. Bottles, small boxes, rolls of bandage, cotton.

"But I'm only a poor fisherman," said father. "I'm not a doctor."

Verl remembered how Miss Arletta, the nurse at the

Veri helped his father lift the injured pilot out of the plane and onto the komatik. The bleeding flyer asked the rescuers to get the first-aid kit.

nursing station, had used the bandages to dress the dog bite on his hand.

"I 'lows I can try," said Verl.

Father held the lantern while Verl laid back the pilot's clothing to bandage the wound, but the bleeding continued. In a very short time the bandages were completely saturated.

"It's no use," said father. "Wrap 'im up good. We'll take 'im to the station."

Verl covered the wound with the remaining bandages, replaced the clothing, and covered the pilot snugly with the robes on the komatik.

Father gave the signal to the dogs, and away went Smut and his followers back over the snowy trail toward home.

Father and Verl were both silent as they rode along. It did not seem so cold, for the wind was now to their backs.

An airplane circled overhead, flying quite low with a deafening roar, then it circled back toward the north and disappeared.

"I 'lows they're looking for the wrecked plane," said father.

"They flew low enough so they could see this is only a dog team," said Verl.

"Wonder 'ow 'e is?" said father. Then he called to the dogs to stop. He lifted the heavy robe and saw that the pilot appeared to be sleeping. Father replaced the cover and stepped on the back of the komatik.

"Yi, Smut, go 'ome," he called, and off they started. "Rada, rada." The dogs made a left turn to avoid some bare rocks.

When they arrived at the nursing station, kind hands assisted father and Verl in lifting the pilot from the komatik and getting him to a bed.

Miss Arletta carefully examined the man for a few moments. Then she turned to father and Verl, saying, "You did all you could. I am sure if he had lived he would have thanked you in person."

Father and Verl found it hard to believe that the pilot was dead.

"I 'lows I didn't do it right," said Verl, referring to the bandages. "Wish I knew 'ow." He stood for a few minutes looking down at the form of the airplane pilot before him. In a flash Verl caught the challenge. He could see the great need for trained men who could "do it right" when an emergency comes.

"Father," said Verl, "if I were a doctor I could 'ave 'elped 'im. Someday I'm going 'outside' to college to be a doctor. I want to travel all up and down the coast 'elping our people."

"That would be fine, my son," said father. "I 'lows I'd be proud of you."

Arriving home, they unharnessed the dogs and secured them in their sheltered kennels. Verl gave them some food while father shook the snow out of the heavy robes.

Mother and Sharna were waiting up for them. There was a warm fire in the stove, and a kettle of hot soup was welcome. Father and Verl soon began to feel comfortable.

"Tell us about it," begged Sharna.

Usually the menfolk related their experiences in a vivid way; but this time neither father nor Verl said much. They stated the bare facts and then were silent. Father placed his empty soup bowl on the table, arose from his chair, and stood looking out of the double window at the snow outside.

Verl took off his boots, said, "Good night," and went upstairs to bed. It was long past midnight.

"I 'lows it's bedtime for you, too, Sharna," said mother.

Three Stories

B USY children were bending over their school desks; some were matching number cards, others were writing in their workbooks, and the older boys were writing English compositions. Teacher had written a topic on the blackboard and had offered a prize to the one who could make the best story from the beginning she had suggested: "Harry stored away his cod traps. 'No more fishing for me,' he said. So he—"

As Tommy bent over his writing he was certain he had a good ending. Perhaps his story would win the prize. Bobby also felt confident that his story would be chosen as the best.

Verl was not writing. He was looking out the window at the long icicles hanging from the roof. Then he turned back to the clean sheet of paper before him, for he realized that the time was passing, and soon teacher would be calling for the stories. Again he read the lines on the blackboard and copied them carefully on his paper. For several minutes Verl continued writing. When teacher called for the papers, Verl was ready to hand his in.

"I will check these stories," teacher said. "Then you may read them aloud to the class after dinner. Your ability to read them well also affects the grade you receive, and I want all of you to decide which story is best."

The children were excited during the noon hour as they thought of judging the stories. This was a new experience for them. Of course, teacher would be the final judge to award the prize.

"I 'ope Tommy wins," was the sentiment of many of the children.

"I think Bobby will win," said Don. " 'Is story is the longest."

Ken was about to say he hoped that Verl would be the winner, but he remembered that Verl had spent half of his time looking out the window.

When the time came for the reading of the compositions, the children sat up straight, with hands clasped on the desks. They were excited and eager. Not a sound was heard as teacher announced, "We will now listen as Bobby reads his story."

Bobby was a bit shy, but he swallowed hard, brushed his hair from his eyes, and stood before the school.

"Harry stored away his cod traps. 'No more fishing for me,' he said. So he put his clothes in a bag and went down to the wharf and got on a boat bound for White Lake.

" 'I am going to the iron mines to work,' said Harry.

"He worked all summer. It was hard work, but he made piles of money. He came away with hundreds of dollars.

" 'What are you going to do with all that money?' one of the miners asked him.

" 'I am going to buy new clothes and give presents to my friends,' said Harry.

"On the way home the boat stopped at Wolf's Head overnight. Harry and some of his friends went into a saloon, and after a spree of drinking and gambling he found that his money was all gone. In the morning the boat came home. Harry did not have any more money, so he had to go back to fishing after all."

The teacher smiled as Bobby placed his paper on the desk and sat down.

"Now we will hear Tommy's story," said the teacher.

Tommy almost strutted up to the front of the room, so confident was he that his story was better than Bobby's. He cleared his throat, straightened the collar of his checkered shirt, and began to read:

"Harry stored away his cod traps. 'No more fishing for me,' he said. He told his mother, 'I'm going to White Lake to work in the iron mines.'

"His mother did not want him to go. Since his father and his grandfather and his great-grandfather had been fishermen, she said he should stay in the village and be a fisherman, too.

"But Harry wanted to go to the mines and get a lot of money. He had said, 'No more fishing for me,' and he meant it.

"On the day he planned to go, the waves in the bay tossed the boat around like a cork. It was a frightful trip, but they finally came to White Lake.

"Harry was almost sick when they got there. He could hardly eat, and the grub was terrible. He tried to work in the mines, but the work nearly killed him. Finally he took the first boat that was going home. " 'Mother,' he said, 'I'll never, never leave home again.' So he had to come back to fishing after all!"

"You may read yours now, Verl," said teacher.

Verl arose clumsily, for he was shy and embarrassed.

"But, teacher," he began, "mine is not like theirs. I 'lows I better wait and write another one. Mine is different."

But the teacher said, "No, Verl, you need not write another one. You have a good story, even though it is different. You may read it now."

Verl hesitated. He looked at the waiting children. Ken and Don were watching him. Sharna and Poggy were eager with anticipation. Even little Lolo was smiling up at him encouragingly.

Verl heaved a sigh, shifting from one foot to the other. Slowly he went to the front of the room, unfolded his paper, and read:

"Harry stored away his cod traps. 'No more fishing for me,' he said. So he put his clothes in a small traveling bag and said good-by to his family. He went down to the wharf and boarded a ship leaving for Canada. He was going to do something that few of his friends had done. He was going 'outside' to get an education. He was not satisfied to stop at the seventh grade, because he could see a great need for doctors in his village. He was going to college to become a doctor.

"One night when the weather was cold, Harry and his father had taken the dog team and komatik to a place where an airplane had crashed in a storm. The pilot was still alive, but he was bleeding. Harry tried to stop the blood with bandages, but he did not know how to do it. The hospital was far away, so the pilot died. Harry decided to learn to be a doctor, so he could come back and help his people.

"Harry did not go back to fishing. He learned to be a doctor. When he came back to his village he traveled up and down the coast helping his people."

Verl finished his story, handed the paper to the teacher, and took his seat. There was not a sound from the children for a few moments. Then they began to whisper to one another. This was a different ending from what they had expected. The teacher sensed the reason for the silence and she said, "Will the three boys leave the room while we vote for the one we think has written the best composition?"

The three boys left the room while the votes were cast. It took longer than usual for the children to make their decisions. Finally the votes were counted.

"You may call them in, now, Poggy," said teacher.

When the three boys had returned to their seats, teacher said, "We find that Verl has the most votes, so the prize will be given to him."

She took a small package from her desk and handed it to the winner. Verl opened it and showed the class a beautiful automatic pencil and a box of leads to use with it.

"Thank you," he stammered.

When the children were on their way home they discussed the three stories.

"But I think Tommy had the best story," said one.

"I thought Bobby's was the best," argued another.

"Verl's was all right, but he said the boy was going

'outside' to college. It might be all right in a story, but if it was real, he'd come back and go fishing as the others did."

The discussion continued in the homes. In most cases the parents agreed that the boy in the story would eventually come back to the village on the coast.

No fire had been built when the children arrived at school. When a fire was started, the students pulled their desks up to the stove to absorb its heat.

An Unexpected Visit

A LIGHT snow had fallen during the night. The children came with their sleds and komatiks across the coves, over the ice, then up over the hills and rocks toward the schoolhouse. When they reached the school on this particular morning they were surprised to find no friendly smoke coming from the chimney. There was no fire in the stove that so often sent out a ruddy glow to make the room warm and cozy.

The "father of the week" was trying to build the fire with wet wood. Teacher was sweeping the snow out of the entry. Some of the children were picking up papers that were strewn over the floor.

"Better leave your coats on until the room is warm," said teacher.

" 'Ow did the snow get in?" asked Don.

"Some persons broke into the schoolhouse last night and did a lot of mischief," explained the teacher. "They left the door open, and the snow blew in. Our firewood was all wet and covered with snow."

"Must 'ave been that gang of 'oodlums," said Ken. "They 'ave been doing mischief all over the village."

"I am not sure," said Verl, "but I 'lows it was that gang of 'oodlums that turned my dogs loose the day they got in our 'ouse and ate up all the dinner. But we can't do a thing. They know there isn't a law to stop 'em. They jes' do as they please."

The "father of the week" sent to the nearest house for a bottle of kerosene, which he dribbled onto the clammy logs. The children pulled their desks near the stove in order to absorb the heat.

"It's so cold in 'ere, I 'lows it's down to zero outside," offered Ken.

"I 'ave to thaw out my 'ands so I can 'old my pencil," said Poggy.

The children did their best to prepare the lessons for the day. About ten o'clock they were able to move their desks away from the stove and take off their overcoats.

Verl seemed to be quite busy looking through his desk. He was evidently searching for something. He looked between the leaves of his books, in his pockets, under the desk, in the bookcase.

"Is there something wrong, Verl?" asked the teacher, noticing his anxiety.

"I can't find the pencil—the one you gave me as a prize. I 'lows it should be 'ere somewhere. I'm sure I 'ad it in my desk."

The other children joined in the search, but the missing pencil was nowhere to be found.

"I have also lost several pages from my notebook," said teacher. "I am sorry that the members of that gang of hoodlums have no respect for the property of others. If they ever should go out into the world they will find themselves out of line with civilization, unless they learn to adjust themselves here. They must learn the necessary lesson of obedience to authority. We will keep the schoolhouse locked from now on to keep out the hoodlums."

Sealing Time

URING the noon hour Verl and Tommy ran to the post office to see if the mail had come. "Hi, Uncle Joe," greeted Verl as he opened the door. Uncle Joe was sitting in his wheel chair in his usual place by the table.

" 'As the mail come in yet?" asked Verl, warming his hands by the stove.

"No," answered Uncle Joe. "The mail boat will not be coming in for a while. But every Friday, weather permitting, the mail plane will fly over and drop the first-class mail as it did last winter. Packages and papers will come from the airport at Echo Point by dog team."

Poor Uncle Joe! How he must miss those weekly treks by dog team to Echo Point to get the mail sacks! How monotonous it must be to sit day after day in a wheel chair and watch other men go out to sea in the fishing boats! Uncle Joe was a strong, healthy man, yet he was a cripple and not able to go fishing.

"How's the family, Verl?" asked Uncle Joe, trying to appear sociable.

"I 'lows we're all right," said Verl.

"And your family, Tommy?" queried Uncle Joe.

"Just fine," said Tommy. "That is, mother and I are. Father went with the sealing boats, but I 'lows 'e will be coming 'ome soon."

"The sealing boats came in this morning," said Uncle Joe. "They're down at the wharf now, unloading. Wish I were able to 'elp them."

"Sealing boats are in!" beamed Tommy. "Good-by, Uncle Joe." In a brief moment the two boys were running over the snow toward the wharf.

Sealing was an exciting time at Rocky Bay. It began when the first cold weather came. The men went out in groups to set their seal traps. Then, when the opportunity came, they returned and brought out the seal, putting them in large seal-fishing boats to bring them home.

" 'Ow many did you get this time?" called Tommy to one of the men who was pulling a big sled full of seals across the snow.

"We got fifty this time," the man called back. "I 'lows we'll get a good price for the fat and skins when we send them down the coast to the plant. We should get forty cents a gallon for the oil."

Verl watched the men unloading the seals from the boat, while Tommy talked with his father. Verl listened as the men called back and forth to each other while they worked.

"I 'lows there'll be plenty of meat to feed the dogs this winter," said one of the men.

"After we get our choice cuts," said another.

"I wish Ken and Don could see the men unload the seals. Poggy would enjoy it, too," said Verl.

"Say, I forgot! We are supposed to be in school. It must be time for the bell," said Tommy.

The boys hurried back to the schoolhouse. They were late, but tardiness was not unusual. If an older child was needed at home to help with the work, he was kept at home. It mattered little to the parents whether he was absent or tardy.

Teacher was passing out the art paper and tempera colors for the painting lesson when the boys came in. They pulled off their jackets and caps, and placed their mittens on the floor near the stove where they would be warm and dry when school was out.

"Today I am going to let you choose the subject you wish to paint," said the teacher. "It may be an object in this room, or something you have in your home. You may draw or paint a fish, an animal, or a bird. There are several books of patterns here on my desk that you may use if you wish."

Verl raised his hand. "Do you 'ave any patterns of seals? I think I will draw a seal on my paper."

"That will be fine, Verl. I think there are patterns for seals in the book with the blue cover."

Tommy raised his hand. "Teacher, did you know that the sealing boats came in? My father came 'ome with them."

"No," said the teacher. "I did not know. But I can imagine you are glad to have your father back home again."

It was difficult for the children to settle down to painting. They were thinking of the excitement down at the wharf. It seemed that the minutes just dragged by.

Sharna was the last one to decide on what to make.

She listened to the swish, swish of paint brushes on the desks around her; but she could not think of a subject to draw. Suddenly a wonderful thought came to her, if only she could put it on paper.

"I 'lows I could never make it look as it really is," she sighed as she traced the outline with her pencil. "Only *He* could do it right."

Slowly, cautiously Sharna applied the water colors, but there was not time to finish before teacher tapped the bell.

"It is time to put your work aside. You may finish your pictures tomorrow," said teacher. "Place your papers on the table here to dry. It is time now for primary reading. The older pupils may work on their spelling."

Sharna put her picture carefully on the table, hoping the colors would not run. She washed out her brushes, closed the lids of her paint jars tightly, and opened her spelling book. She tried to wipe off the stains of red, orange, and yellow paint from her fingers. Perhaps they would come off in the dishwater that night.

As soon as school was dismissed that afternoon, the boys raced down to the wharf. The girls trudged home, for they had certain tasks to do to help mother.

"Did you finish your picture?" asked Sharna.

"Not quite," said LuDell.

"I didn't finish mine, either," admitted Sharna. "What did you make?"

"I made a dog team and a komatik," said LuDell. "Maybe I can finish it tomorrow. What did you make?"

"I 'lows it doesn't look much like anything yet," said Sharna. "It's all just a big smear of yellow and orange and red. But when it is finished, I 'ope it looks like the sunset from Lookout Rock. What are you making, Lolo?"

"Oh, not much—just a pretty doll like the one I want for Christmas."

"With brown 'air?" asked Sharna.

"No, yellow 'air, and a blue dress," said Lolo.

"I 'lows Christmas will soon be 'ere," said LuDell. "We're going to 'ave a lot of get-togethers. Won't we 'ave fun?"

"I 'ope we 'ave a good Christmas," said Sharna. "Teacher says the real meaning of Christmas is so mixed up with merriment that many people forget the birthday of the One we wish to honor."

"That is what my grandmother said, too," said LuDell.

"The Christmas carols will 'elp us remember," said Sharna. "We are going to learn a new one tomorrow."

Wolves Along the Trail

IT WAS a bright sunny morning when a group of men and boys started out for the woods with their komatiks and dog teams to get fuel. "Ugh, ugh!" shouted the men to the lead dogs, and away went the teams along the paths. How the dogs leaped and ran in the snow!

"Better take it easy," said father. "I 'lows you'll be all tired out before we get halfway there. Slow down, Smut. Take it easy, Blackie."

The komatiks followed one behind the other in a train. The men and boys of the village spent much of their time in the woods cutting trees and trimming the logs. They took supplies with them and camped at night in shacks or cabins. Sometimes they stacked up the logs and left them until spring. Some of the older boys had to miss school for a few days to help in the woods. Verl and Tommy were getting big and strong, so they were expected to do their share of the hard work.

All day the sounds of axes and saws sent echoes ringing through the timber. As the sun was setting, father said to Verl, "I 'lows you and Tommy better feed your dogs and get a bite to eat yourselves. Then start for 'ome with your loads. It'll be late before you get there, any-way. I tied your load on good. So 'urry now."

The two boys did as they were told. Tommy was in the lead with Verl close behind, calling to his dogs, "Ugh, ugh; rada, rada!"

The sun had set when they passed through Echo Point. The wind was at their backs as they headed south across the crisp snow toward Rocky Bay.

"Only eight more miles," called Verl to Tommy.

"I 'lows we'll get 'ome around nine o'clock," Tommy called back.

It was a cold, crisp night. Stars were shining in the blue canopy overhead. The moon was bright, though it was not yet full. It seemed like a tiny boat sailing along in a sea of blue.

Verl was thinking of some of the things Sharna had told him about God and the beauties of nature. The teacher read many passages from the Bible for the open-ing exercises at school. The children had memorized Psalm 27.

"I wish I knew more about the heavenly Father," mused Verl, as he listened to the steady crunching of the komatik runners on the snow. "I wish I could know for sure that He is real as teacher says, and that He answers our prayers. Sharna believes, but she is just a little girl. Yet sometimes I think she knows more about some things than I do. Yi, Smut, Blackie! Steady there, Jip. Keep going, or you'll tangle your traces."

Tommy also was calling to his dogs. They had slowed

up and stopped. They seemed to be either tired or nervous, for they did not want to go on.

"What's the matter?" asked Verl.

"They've lost the way, maybe?" said Tommy questioningly. "I 'lows you better take the lead. Your dog Smut knows the way down between the cliffs."

"We can try," said Verl, urging on the dogs, around Tommy's team and breaking a fresh track in the snow. "Come on, Smut; go 'ome!"

For several minutes the dogs ran steadily. Then suddenly Smut stopped, and the other dogs did likewise.

"I 'lows maybe the load is too 'eavy," said Tommy.

"I don't think so," said Verl. "They've pulled bigger loads than this."

Suddenly from somewhere in the darkness came the unmistakable call of a timber wolf.

"Did you 'ear that?" he asked.

"I 'eard it before—when the dogs stopped the first time," said Tommy.

"Let's get going," said Verl. " 'Ome, Smut; 'ome as fast as you can!"

Over the snow they went again. To Verl and Tommy, the teams seemed crawling along, so eager were they to reach the village before the wolves discovered their trail.

Verl thought he heard an answer to the wolf call, and fear came into his heart as he thought of the stories he had heard of narrow escapes of the men of the village who had been attacked by wolf packs.

The call came again from the north. It was answered by an eerie call from the direction of the cliffs. Verl knew Tommy had heard it, for the boy was urging his team on almost frantically.

The wolf calls echoed and re-echoed as Verl and Tommy went down the trail in the moonlight. Verl began to whistle and then to sing. He was no longer afraid.

Verl remembered a verse of one of the psalms he had
learned at school. "He shall call upon Me, and I will
answer him: I will be with him in trouble; I will deliver
him, and honor him." (Psalm 91:15.)

Verl looked up into the starry heavens. Somewhere
up beyond the stars was the loving Father, a God who
cared for His children. He was waiting for them to call
upon Him in their time of need.

"Please don't let the wolves 'urt Tommy or me or the
dogs. 'Elp us to get 'ome safe."

Then he called again to the dogs, and it seemed to
the youth that they resumed their normal speed as they
raced lightly across the snow. Tommy's dog team followed close behind.

The wolf calls echoed and re-echoed as the boys went
down the cliff trail, but somehow Verl was no longer
afraid. He began to whistle, then to sing. It was not a
cowboy song that he sang, but one of the hymns he had
often sung in the church on the hill, a song of praise
and deliverance.

> When in distress and greatest fear
>   We lift our voices high,
> O holy God, omnipotent,
>   Thou art forever nigh.
> O Thou who reignest high above,
>   Beyond the starry sky,
> All praise and glory be to Thee,
>   Who hears our faintest cry.
> For Thou wilt answer when I call,
>   Wherever I may be.
> In time of trouble Thou wilt hear
>   And wilt deliver me.

Verl had sung that hymn as Aunt Minnie played it on

the wheezy organ at church, but tonight it had a new meaning for him. The ominpotent Father *was* real; He *did* answer prayers. As the few scattered lights of the village of Rocky Bay came into view, Verl knew that God was real.

They were home at last, safe from a possible attack from the wolves that called back and forth to each other across the vast expanse of snow.

Tommy followed Verl as far as Lookout Rock. There the two dog teams stopped, and Tommy said,

"I 'lows we got 'ome safe. The wolves didn't get us."

"Yes," said Verl, "but it was the ominpotent Father that kept them from even chasing us."

" 'Ow do you know?" asked Tommy.

"Because I asked Him," said Verl in a definite way, "and He answered my prayer. That's 'ow I know."

"Well, good night, Verl," said Tommy as he started the komatik down the path to his home. Tommy was thoughtful as he unharnessed the dogs and tied them securely in their shelters. He was thinking about the ride home from Echo Point. How frightened he had been! Verl had faith to believe that God would take care of them, and he had prayed. It was something for Tommy to think about long after he was safe in bed.

Verl secured the dogs in their kennels, gave them some food, then unloaded the wood from the big komatik and piled it up in a sheltered place where it would keep dry. It was late when he entered the house. Mother and Sharna were still up. Sharna was holding a skein of yarn while mother rolled it into a ball.

"Is everything all right, Verl?" asked mother, as Verl hung his coat near the stove to dry. "If you are 'ungry, there's some 'ot stew for you on the back of the stove."

"I 'lows I am a bit 'ungry," admitted Verl. Then while he ate his bowl of stew he gave an account of his experience on the way home.

Sharna sat on a chair across the table, not missing a single word. She loved her big brother; she, too, had prayed for his safety that night on his trek home.

"I was afraid you might 'ave got lost," said Sharna, "or that you would get your feet frozen as Uncle Joe did, and 'ave to sit in a wheel chair. But I 'lows wolves would be even worse. It is as teacher said: The holy omnipotent Father does take care of us any time we ask Him to help us."

"Yes," mused Verl. "I know that God is real, and I am going to serve Him from now on with all my 'eart."

Mother's heart was stirred by what she heard. She recalled the story the teacher told of the love of God. Never before had the heavenly Father seemed so real and personal. Wolves were on the trail, calling back and forth to each other; yet the boys had not been attacked.

"If only I could read," mother sighed wearily as she crawled into bed. "But I 'lows my children will 'ave an education, even if I couldn't. Thank You, God, for sending us a Christian teacher."

Poor Old Smut

SHARNA! Sharna! Wait for me," called a familiar voice. The girl turned to see Poggy coming behind her, running as fast as his chubby legs could carry him.

It was a cold, clear Friday afternoon. School had been dismissed, and the children were on their way to the post office to wait for the mail. Word had come through the teleghraph office that the mail planes would drop first-class mail on Fridays, weather permitting. The children were eager to see the big red plane that would fly overhead and drop the mail sack, so they hurried down to the pole near the center of the village.

"There's Uncle Rex now!" said Sharna to LuDell and Lolo. "Hurry, Poggy. I 'lows it's time for the plane. The red flag is going up!"

Somewhat out of breath, Poggy joined the girls, and they all ran down the path to where the group of boys and girls had gathered.

" 'Ow did Uncle Rex know the plane was coming?" asked Lolo.

"Somebody telegraphed him," Sharna explained. "Listen! I 'ear it coming." Sharna shaded her eyes as she looked up into the sky, trying to discover the plane that was flying across the bay toward them.

"I 'ear it, too," beamed Poggy. "It's a plane, all right. I 'lows it's going to fly right over our 'eads."

Sharna and LuDell began jumping up and down. "It's the mail plane!" they cried excitedly. "It's the mail plane!"

At first the plane flew directly over the group; then it circled around and flew lower and lower.

The children held their mittened hands over their ears as the plane roared low over their heads. The mail bag was dropped somewhere near the pole, and the plane quickly vanished in low clouds as it headed for Echo Point.

Uncle Rex carried the mail sack down to the post office and delivered it to Aunt Minnie.

"I 'lows we'll 'ave to wait till Uncle Joe sorts it out before we get ours," said Sharna.

Suddenly Poggy gave five shrill whistles through his teeth. From beyond the flagpole came one long whistle in answer.

"It's Verl," said Sharna to LuDell. "Poggy is signaling to 'im. I wonder where 'e is going?"

"I'll find out," said Poggy, and away he went to join his big brother.

"Where are you going?" he asked as he scrambled up over the rocks.

"To the nursing station," answered Verl.

"Got another dog bite?" asked Poggy. "Where? Let's see it."

"No, I didn't get bit," said Verl.

"What's wrong?" Poggy said with a puzzled look.

"Why am I going to the nursing station?" Verl helped Poggy with his question. "To see if Miss Arletta can do something for the dogs. Tommy's father says they will all get it if they aren't vaccinated."

"Get what?" asked Poggy.

"Distemper. That's what so many of the dogs around 'ere 'ave been dying of, and some of our dogs are sick."

"Which ones?" Poggy was quite concerned. "Not Smut or Blackie, I 'ope."

"Yes, Smut and Blackie, Cash and Boots," said Verl. "Snap and Jip are not well, and even old Sade won't eat."

For several days Miss Arletta was a busy nurse. The government had sent the vaccine; and because Miss Arletta was the only person in the village qualified to give the shots to the dogs, the task was assigned to her.

With the help of Tommy's father and Verl, she vaccinated nearly all the dogs in the village. The men knew how to manage the dogs, so she had no trouble. Even old Sade's little puppies had their shots.

But for many of the dogs the serum was given too late. One morning Verl came into the house with a sad expression on his face. Mother noticed it and asked, "Is it bad, son?"

For a moment Verl could not speak. Finally he said, "Poor old Smut—'e was the best lead dog we 'ad, too."

" 'Ow about the puppies?" asked Ken.

"I 'lows I won't 'ave them very long either," said Verl as he wiped his hands on the family towel and took his place at the breakfast table.

" Ow about the little black one?" asked Poggy.

" 'E's as frisky as ever," said Verl. "But one of the spotted ones and the white one I gave to teacher—they're both dead."

Sharna looked up from her bowl of cereal. There were tears in her eyes as she asked, "Why do puppies 'ave to die?"

No one seemed to know the answer. Each member of the family finished his breakfast and left the room.

That afternoon out on Lookout Rock, Sharna and LuDell talked about it. LuDell was quite emphatic when she said, "I told you long ago that God takes away your breath when you die. He's the One who killed all the dogs—even the puppies. Many people in the village say so."

"But LuDell, don't you remember what teacher said? The omnipotent Father loves us, and He takes care of us. He wants us to be 'appy. He wouldn't kill the dogs; He made them."

"Yes, I know," said LuDell. "I was saying what the people in the village are saying. Let's not quarrel, Sharna. You are my best friend. Let's go to the post office. I think the dog teams came in from Echo Point with the second-class mail. Did you get your new mail-order catalogue? Last week there were twelve bags of catalogues delivered."

"Yes, we got ours," said Sharna. "Did I tell you what mother did about a month ago?"

"No, what?" queried LuDell.

"From our old catalogue she ordered the most beautiful doll for Lolo. It has a blue bonnet and dress, and yellow 'air. But Aunt Minnie is keeping it under 'er bed until Christmas."

" 'Ow did your Aunt Minnie know the package 'ad a doll in it?" asked LuDell.

"When it came she lifted it up to see who it was for, and she 'eard it say 'Ma-ma.' She knew it was the doll mother ordered for Lolo. You won't tell, will you?"

"Of course not," promised LuDell, " 'cause I'm your best friend. What do you want for Christmas?"

"Oh, I 'lows I'll be 'appy with anything I get," said Sharna.

Christmas at Rocky Bay

FOR several days the red line in the thermometer had gone down below the zero mark. The wind roared wildly, making the frosted windows snap and rattle in their frames. A heavy snow had fallen, covering the village of Rocky Bay with a thick white blanket; and the wind had drifted and piled the snow around the homes so that it was difficult for people to get from place to place. Boats could not come into the icebound harbor. Planes could not fly in the stormy weather. The village was shut away from the outside world by a white curtain, which only the battery radios could penetrate.

"Turn on a story," said Ken, as he stretched out on his favorite rug.

"I 'lows there won't be any Westerns today," said mother. "This is Christmas."

As Verl turned the dial, holiday music filled the air. The children were busy with their gifts. Verl had some new books to read; Ken and Don had jigsaw puzzles to put together; and Poggy played with a small wind-up train on metal tracks. Sharna and Lolo were busy dressing and undressing their new dolls.

Father was out in the kitchen watching mother roll out the piecrust. It was good to be at home again with the family. They had so much to talk about, so much to enjoy together! Let the snow and wind blow around the house; it was cozy and warm inside.

"Father—" It was Sharna standing by his side, holding her new doll in her hands.

"What's the trouble, Sharna?" asked father.

"My new doll— See? The arm came off."

Father pretended he was a doctor in a big hospital.

"I 'lows I'll 'ave to operate immediately," he said, trying to look solemn. "I'll 'ave the nurse get 'er ready for the operating room."

"Father, you are so funny!" laughed Sharna. "I love you so much, and when you play with us this way, I love you so much more!" Sharna put her arms around father's neck and kissed him on the cheek.

"Careful, now," said father playfully; "you must not interfere with this serious operation."

In no time at all, it seemed, father reached inside the body cavity and drew out the heavy rubber and fastened it back on the hook at the shoulder. With a pair of pliers he tightened the hook.

"I 'lows she'll live now, little mother," he said, "but take good care of 'er from now on."

"Thank you." And away ran Sharna to show Lolo that her doll was as good as new again.

Suddenly there was a rap on the door.

"Now, who would come out in a storm like this?" inquired mother.

Father opened the door. "Come in!" he said. The visitor was bundled up against the weather with a heavy scarf tied over the face. Mother wiped the flour from her hands and helped remove the snow-covered scarf and parka.

"Eulene!" exclaimed mother. "Why did you come out in a storm like this? 'Ere, sit down by the stove. You must be nearly frozen!"

The children came out into the kitchen to welcome their cousin, Eulene, with the cheery greeting, "Merry Christmas!"

Eulene did not say a word, for she was having difficulty in breathing, and her eyes were red from crying.

"Eulene, dear," said mother kindly, putting her arm around her, "tell your Auntie Lou what the trouble is."

Eulene only burst into tears again, and she buried her face in her hands and sobbed piteously.

"Now, now," said mother soothingly, "I 'lows nothing can be that bad." Then she turned to her family and motioned for them to go into the other room. When the door between the two rooms was closed, mother gently drew the story from Eulene, bit by bit between sobs.

"I wish I'd never gone 'outside,' " said Eulene, "and I wish I'd not come back. Nobody wants me any more —not 'outside' or here. Nobody loves me—nobody!"

Mother patted Eulene's shoulder. It wasn't going to be easy to reason with this unhappy young girl who was so misunderstood.

"What about your father and mother?" asked mother. "Surely you believe they love you. And Uncle Rex and Aunt Carol and the children; you have been staying with them since you came back."

"But I can't stay there any more. I was not happy there, and besides, they have enough mouths to feed without mine."

"But *we* love you," said mother. "We can keep you 'ere for a while until you decide to go back to your folks."

"Oh, Auntie Lou," sobbed Eulene, "you're so kind. I just couldn't bother you, and I can't go back to my folks, either."

"Now stop your crying 'fore you make yourself sick. This is Christmas Day, and you should be 'appy."

"How can I be happy when the people in the village are all talking about me? They say I'm different since I went away. Do you think I'm different, Auntie Lou?"

Eulene lifted her eyes to her aunt. Yes, two years in the "outside" world had made her different; she was more mature, more like the others who had come from "outside." Yet today she was just a lonely, disappointed girl.

"I 'lows you 'ave changed a little, dear; but we love you just the same. The heavenly Father loves you most of all, and He'll work things out for you. Come now, we should not be sad on Christmas. Wash your face and dry your tears; then see what the children are doing in the other room. I 'lows they want to show you what they got for Christmas."

Sharna seemed to sense that Eulene needed someone to make her forget her troubles, and by the time mother announced dinner, Eulene was laughing merrily as she joined in playing games with the children. Sharna had never really known her cousin Eulene, for she was older and had gone away before Sharna had grown up enough to become well acquainted. During the afternoon,

Sharna discovered that Eulene was lots of fun. She
played with the dolls, helped the boys with their puzzles,
and made a tiny engineer out of paper for Poggy's toy
train. That night, after the supper dishes were washed
and put away, the family settled down in the living
room to listen to Christmas music on the radio. Somehow the familiar carols put the family in a pensive mood.
Mother sat quietly in her favorite chair with her knitting.
The four boys stretched out in their usual places on the
floor, while Sharna and Lolo sat on their stools holding
their new dolls. Eulene seemed to be somehow apart
from this happy family. She sat stiffly on a chair looking
first at one and then another. Sharna noticed the for-
lorn expression on her cousin's face. How terrible it
must be to be so lonely!

"Eulene," invited Sharna, "bring your chair over
'ere and sit with us."

Eulene seemed to brighten up in an instant. She
carried her chair to the other side of the room and sat
between Sharna and Lolo.

"Let's sing with the radio," suggested Sharna. "We
learned some of those carols in school."

"You really like school, don't you, Sharna?" asked
Eulene.

"Yes, very much," admitted Sharna. "We 'ave a nice
teacher, too. She's from the 'outside.' "

"So I've heard," said Eulene.

"Sometimes she reads wonderful stories to us," continued Sharna, "and she taught us to sing together, just
like a choir."

As Sharna paused to hum along with the Christmas
carol that was coming from the radio, Eulene joined her.

Before the first stanza of the song was completed, the boys added their voices,

"... and heaven and nature sing."

Father and mother had never heard the children sing together that way, and they smiled their approval. As Verl's voice came out deep and strong, they realized that he was almost a man. On and on the children sang until the program was ended. They listened a few moments to the weather report stating that tomorrow would be clear and warmer.

"I 'lows it will be a nice day," said father. "Perhaps the men will go out again with the seal nets. But, now, 'ow about going to bed?"

Mother laid aside her knitting and said, "I'll make up a bed on the cot for Lolo. Eulene can sleep with Sharna."

"I'll check the dogs," said Verl.

"I'll go tonight," said father.

"No, father, I'll go," said Verl. "You stay where it's warm."

"I 'lows we can both go, then," said father. "We can each bring in a load of logs."

Ken, Don, and Poggy were already upstairs, having a race to see who would be the first one in bed. "Last one ready 'as to blow out the light," said Ken.

Sharna and Eulene climbed the stairs to their bedroom. "This 'as been a wonderful Christmas Day," said Sharna. "I'm glad you came to be with us."

"I've enjoyed it, too," said Eulene. "I never had any sisters or brothers. I wish I belonged to a family like yours."

"You belong to Uncle Tom and Auntie Lil. They

really missed you when you went away. And you belong to the omnipotent Father, too," said Sharna.

Sharna blew out the light and knelt beside the bed to pray. Eulene waited—it seemed such a long time. When Sharna snuggled down between the covers, Eulene asked, "Do you always say your prayers, Sharna?"

"Yes, ever since I can remember."

"I used to," said Eulene; "but since I went 'outside' and worked with the other girls, well, I got out of the habit. None of the factory girls say their prayers. They never talk about God except when they swear. It really shocked me at first, but I got used to it. My folks were very strict. That's why I don't want to stay home with them. They don't understand me, and even Uncle Rex and Aunt Carol think I'm a heathen. I can't stay with them any more. Don't get me wrong, Sharna, they asked me to stay, but I'm not happy there."

"You still believe in the omnipotent Father, don't you, Eulene?"

"Yes, in a way," agreed the cousin.

"And you believe He made the world and all the wonderful things in it, don't you?"

"Yes."

"Then I 'lows you believe that He loves you, and He wants you to love Him with all your 'eart. You do, don't you, Eulene?" asked Sharna.

For several minutes there was silence. Then a faint sob came from the pillow.

"Please, Eulene, don't cry. I know you love God. He will make everything come out all right. We just 'ave to trust Him."

Sharna felt an arm reaching toward her under the

covers. Eulene gave her a tight squeeze. "Sharna, you will never know how much you've helped me. Tomorrow I'm going home—to my home. I want to make it all up to my folks. But first, I have something to do, something I have not done for a long time." Eulene crawled out of bed and knelt on the fur rug beside the bed.

This time Sharna waited. Then she slipped out of bed and knelt beside Eulene.

"It 'as been a wonderful Christmas," said Sharna sleepily, as the girls snuggled in the warm bed, content in the decision that had been made.

Funny Faces

WHAT the weatherman predicted on the radio came true. The weather cleared, and the thermometer began to climb. The villagers shoveled the drifted snow from their doorways so their neighbors could come to visit. From December 25 to January 6, they observed the old custom of mumming. What fun they had going from house to house dressed in strange disguises and masks, having people guess who they were!

"I 'lows they will never guess who I am," said Sharna to LuDell, as she looked up from her painting. "Did you ever see such a funny face?"

"Look at mine," laughed LuDell. "Won't we 'ave fun!"

The two girls were painting queer faces on cardboard cartons. They would cut out holes for eyes, sew sheets to the cartons, and slip them over their heads. It would be almost impossible for their neighbors to recognize them.

"I'll make one for Poggy, and then 'elp Lolo with 'ers," said Sharna.

"I'll 'elp Lolo if you want me to, while you make Poggy's," offered LuDell. "Then we can go up to grandfather's and see if teacher can guess who we are."

The water-color paint dried quickly, and then came the most difficult part of sewing the sheets to the cardboard. But with a little help from mother, the children were ready to go calling.

Over snowbanks and bare rocks they climbed. In some places the drifts were deep, but they plowed through the snow, and, quite out of breath, reached grandfather's house.

Grandfather pretended he was afraid of the funny faces. In spite of their efforts to change their voices, they laughed merrily as they danced around the kitchen. Grandmother and teacher stood by the cupboard and watched. They whispered and nodded to each other. Then teacher said, "I think we know who you are."

The children stopped their dancing, and waited for grandfather to guess first.

"Let me see, now," he began. "I 'lows this one is Bobby, and this is Shirley."

How the children squealed with delight at his wild guesses. He was enjoying the fun as much as they were. Then it was grandmother's turn. She recognized LuDell, but was a bit confused with the others. Finally, teacher pointed each one out correctly. They took off their masks and sat quietly on chairs while grandma passed a plate of cookies.

" 'Ow did you know us, teacher?" asked Sharna.

"Those funny faces did not fool me," she replied. "I

could tell by your voices. I should know you all quite well."

From house to house the children went. There were many family gatherings during the holidays, plenty of good things to eat, and much merrymaking. The children went sliding on hills and snowbanks. They also had good times on their skis, snowshoes, and sleds. The little red line on the thermometer continued to rise higher each day as the wind blew in from the bay instead of from the northwest.

"I 'lows we'll 'ave a January thaw," predicted father one day. "If we do, the mail planes will be recalled because the dog teams won't be able to travel to the airport at Echo Point."

"A lot of the meat will spoil, too," added mother.

"I 'lows we can give it to the dogs," said Verl. "We boys are planning to go hunting across the cove tomorrow."

"Who are you going with?" questioned Poggy.

"Tommy, Bob, and Henry. Maybe we'll take Ken and Don along if they care to go."

"Sure! We'll go!" beamed Ken and Don.

"Maybe I can snare that other rabbit," said Ken, "the one that got away."

"Will we take the big komatik?" asked Don.

"No," said Verl. "We 'ave only five dogs, you know. We'll go with Tommy's dog sled. 'E 'as the best dog team now."

Ken was thinking rather seriously about something. Then he asked, "Do you think it will thaw very much, father? 'Cause if it does, and the ice melts in the cove, we won't be able to get back 'ome with the dog sled!"

"I 'ardly think it will thaw that fast. The ice is thicker

than you think. It won't break up till sometime in March. We'll 'ave more winter yet, you'll see."

And father was right. When the first week in January had passed, the weather grew cold again. The red line in the thermometer almost vanished from sight below the zero mark. Cold winds blew fiercely from the northwest. Snow came whirling around the buildings, stinging the cheeks and nose of anyone who ventured outside.

In March, father went back to the iron mines at White Lake. Sharna was happy that Verl did not go with him. The youth had definitely decided to stay at home and finish the school year. Someday he wanted to go to high school, then to college, and afterward perpare to be a doctor. It would be hard work, he knew; but he could see the need for doctors in that north country. He wanted to be like Sir Wilfred T. Grenfell, who had done so much for the people of Labrador. He, too, would be a missionary in the Far North.

Poggy Rows the Boat in the Landwash

SCHOOL was out for the afternoon. The children went splashing homeward through the slush and mud. Each one had something special to do, it seemed, except Poggy. Verl was going to repack the meat in the icehouse. Ken and Don would fill the water barrel. Sharna was to scrub the kitchen floor that became tracked with mud when the snow melted. Lolo would help mother fold the towels, washcloths, and tea towels.

Since Poggy had no special job assigned to him, he could make his own plans. "I'll take the little boat out on the landwash," he said as he trudged homeward.

"But there are big slabs of ice floating in the water," objected Ken.

"I 'lows I can pull the boat up over the ice and push it down on the other side," boasted Poggy.

"Yes, I 'lows you can," said Ken.

"I'll carry your reading book 'ome for you," offered Sharna.

"Do you want me to 'elp you tip it over so you can spill out the melted snow?" offered Don.

"No, I 'lows I'm strong enough to do that by myself." With a toss of his head away went Poggy to the land-wash.

" 'E's an independent little fellow," said Sharna to LuDell. " 'E will soon be eight years old, and 'e thinks 'e's almost a man."

"As soon as you finish scrubbing," said LuDell, "I'll meet you on Lookout Rock. It is such a nice evening."

"I'll 'urry," said Sharna.

For about an hour Poggy rowed the little boat out in the landwash, between the cakes of ice that floated there. Some were small, some were large. Poggy could row around the small masses of floating drift ice, but when he came to the big ones, he jumped out of the boat onto the ice, pulled the boat up and dragged it across the ice, then let it down on the other side. It was fun! Poggy could hear the shouts of some boys who were playing on the other side of Lookout Rock. They were also in boats splashing about in the landwash.

As Poggy was letting the boat down into the water, somehow the rope by which he pulled the boat slipped out of his mittened hand. Before he could catch it, the boat had drifted beyond his reach. As Poggy stood on the ice, watching the craft going farther and farther from him, he realized that it was not the boat but the cake of drift ice upon which he was standing that was moving. It was going farther out toward the deep water of the bay.

Poggy knew that even if he should take off his heavy outer clothing and plunge into the icy water, he could

Poggy stood on the cake of ice, watching his boat drift beyond his reach. Darkness was coming on, and the boy was floating out to sea on the ice.

not swim, for he had never learned. The little boat was getting smaller and smaller. What if the cake of drift ice should float out beyond the bay into the ocean? What if the ice should melt before somebody came to help him? Even Lookout Rock seemed to be getting smaller and smaller. He thought he saw two people up there, but it might be just bare rocks.

Suddenly Poggy remembered something. Why had he not thought of it before? He pulled off his mittens and held them between his knees while he blew five sharp whistles through his teeth. He waited a moment, then blew five more.

"What's the use?" thought Poggy. "I'm so far away, they can't 'ear me."

He called and called, but only the echoes came back to him from the rocks on shore. He whistled again and waved his arms in the air. He ran back and forth on the drift ice, trying to attract someone's attention.

Maybe one of the boys rowing a boat on the other side of Lookout Rock had seen him. He called again, but only the splashing of the dark water against the edges of the drift ice could be heard in answer. The sun was going down; it would soon be night. Big tears came rolling down Poggy's cheeks. He might never get home again!

Poggy gave five more shrill whistles, and then he buried his face in his mittens and cried. It was no use to whistle or call any more; he was too far away to make anyone hear him.

As he saw the faint outline of Lookout Rock growing dimmer, he suddenly thought of something Sharna had told him. "Whenever you are in trouble, Poggy, pray to the holy omnipotent Father, and He'll 'elp you."

"But I am too far away. Nobody can 'elp me way out 'ere!" he said aloud. "Not even God can see me way out 'ere." The boy lay down on the cold ice and wept.

It was getting dark. The pink and gold in the western sky was fading away. Stars began to appear up in the dark sky above. It was quiet and still! The only sound was the gentle lapping of the water against the ice. The waves rocked the ice like a cradle.

"I'm tired and sleepy," sighed Poggy. "I wish I could go to bed; but I 'lows I just can't go anywhere. It is going to be mighty cold sleeping out 'ere tonight!"

He pulled his jacket collar up around his neck as the wind whipped across the icy water of the bay. He wiped the tears from his eyes with the back of his mitten.

"If I go to sleep, I 'ave to say my prayers first," said Poggy, as he knelt on the ice, folded his mittened hands, and prayed. When he said, "Amen," he lay down again on the ice to go to sleep.

"Maybe the holy omnipotent Father couldn't 'ear me 'way out on this big ocean. But Sharna said He takes care of us wherever we are. But I wish—I wish I could be 'ome in my own, warm bed."

Five Sharp Whistles

SHARNA squeezed out the mop and stood back to admire the spotless kitchen floor that she had finished scrubbing. "Now don't you walk on it, Lolo, till it gets dry. I'm going to Lookout Rock with LuDell. Call me when mother needs me to 'elp 'er get supper, won't you?"

"I'll blow my whistle—six times," said Lolo.

"Remember, don't walk on the floor till it is dry."

Away went Sharna, tying her scarf over her ears as she ran down the path toward Lookout Rock. LuDell was already there, watching the children play in their homemade boats in the landwash.

"Did you get your kitchen floor scrubbed?" asked LuDell.

"Yes, and it looks nice even if I did 'urry. Lolo will call me when mother needs me."

"We 'ad fun in school today," said LuDell. "I got my seeds all planted in cans. I wonder 'ow long it will take for them to grow."

"Teacher said they should grow fast if we keep them

in a sunny place. I put mine on the first window sill by the maps."

"What color did you paint your tin cans?" asked LuDell.

"Red. They'll look pretty when the green leaves begin to show. I 'lows we'll 'ave fun making our flower scrapbooks, too. Teacher gives us such good ideas. She makes a game out of school."

"Listen! I think that is Lolo whistling for me," said Sharna suddenly.

The girls listened.

"No," said Sharna. "That was only five whistles. Lolo 'as six."

"Maybe she did not count right," said LuDell.

"Yes, Lolo knows 'ow to count. That was Poggy."

" 'E's down 'ere in the landwash with the kids. I've been watching them for a long time."   -

But Sharna was not satisfied. She kept her ears alert in case he whistled again.

"There it is!" said Sharna. "Five sharp whistles. That means Poggy is signaling." She stood up and looked down at the children playing tag with their boats, but she did not see Poggy.

Five more whistles came from a distance.

"There 'e is, LuDell," cried Sharna. "See 'im way out there on that cake of drift ice, waving 'is 'ands? 'E's lost 'is boat, and 'e's in trouble."

Sharna put her fingers between her teeth and whistled four times. She whistled again and again, but nobody seemed to answer. Only the merry laughter of the children rowing their boats could be heard.

"LuDell, what can we do? Somebody must go after

'im. 'E's going farther way all the time. If I could row a boat I'd go out there and get 'im. Poor little Poggy."

LuDell shaded her eyes against the setting sun. "What if that piece of drift ice melts, we'll never see 'im again," said LuDell.

" 'Ow can you say that when you see 'e is in trouble? I've got to get 'elp," said Sharna, almost in tears. The girl whistled again and again, but she had no response.

"It's no use," said LuDell. "Nobody can 'elp 'im now. 'E's too far away."

But Sharna knew of One who could help Poggy. She knelt down on the cold, bare rocks and prayed to her heavenly Father.

"Please 'elp 'im. 'E's such a little boy. 'E can't swim, and I can't row a boat. Please send somebody to bring 'im back to us. Amen."

Sharna arose from her knees and whistled again. Somewhere in the distance she thought she heard an answer. There was one, then two, then three distinct answers to her signal. Verl, Ken, and Don were coming.

"Thank You, God," said Sharna reverently, as she looked up into the rosy clouds above the bay. "I knew You would send 'elp if I asked You."

LuDell was touched by the sincerity of her friend and the complete faith she had that God would answer her prayer.

When Verl came near Lookout Rock, Sharna called to him, and pointed out in the bay to where Poggy was on the piece of drift ice. After Ken and Don had helped Verl push out the big boat, they stood by to wait until he returned. Verl thought he could manage the boat better if he were alone in the midst of the floating ice.

"We'll go out after 'is boat," offered Ken. "I can still see it away over there." The excited boy pointed across the water.

"I'll get my boat," said Don.

As Verl rowed he prayed silently that he might be able to reach Poggy before the ice crumbled or before it became too dark to find him.

As he neared the place where he last saw Poggy he gave the signal—one long whistle. From somewhere out beyond a stretch of open water came an answer—five sharp whistles.

"I'm coming, Poggy," called Verl. "Sit tight. I'm coming with the big boat."

From the floating raft of ice not very far away came an answer, "I am sitting tight, Verl. I knew you'd come to get me. Did you find my boat?"

"Don't worry about your boat, Poggy. Ken and Don went out to bring it in."

Verl drew the boat up close against the ice and helped Poggy to climb aboard. "Easy now, Poggy. Don't slip and fall into the water.

"I 'lows you are about froze!" said Verl. " 'Ere, wrap up in my coat. I don't need it, for I am warm from rowing."

As Verl put his coat around the shivering Poggy, he held the little fellow close to him. Poggy burst into tears.

"Don't cry. You're safe now," said Verl.

"But I thought nobody would ever find me 'way out 'ere, and I'd never get 'ome again. I called and whistled for so long. I even said my prayers, but God couldn't 'ear me so far out on the ocean."

"Poggy," said Verl, as he pulled on the oars with a

strong, steady motion, "don't ever forget that the omnipotent Father is always watching you. He'll take care of you, no matter where you are. He could see you out 'ere on the ice and He knew you were afraid and lonely. He 'ad Sharna signal to me, and He sent me out 'ere to get you. I 'ope mother 'as supper ready when we get there. I 'lows you're mighty 'ungry by now."

Poggy did not say a word. He merely nodded his head and tucked his chin down into the collar of Verl's coat.

Mother, Sharna, and Lolo were waiting when Verl and Poggy came ashore. Several of the neighbors had heard of the boy's plight, and were there also, anxiously waiting for the rescue boat to arrive.

"Poor little fellow," said mother, as Verl carried him up to her.

Soon Don came in with his boat, followed by Ken with Poggy's. They fastened the boats at the landing.

" 'E's asleep," said Verl. "I'll carry 'im on up to the 'ouse." The strong youth could tell by her voice that his mother had been crying.

"It's all right now," said Verl. "God took care of 'im and sent me out to save 'im. Someday maybe I will 'ave a chance to save others, like the song we sing in school, 'I will make you fishers of men.' Someday I'll have a big boat and go up and down the coast to 'elp people."

The School Program

FOR many weeks the children of Rocky Bay had been working diligently on their lessons in order to complete the required amount before the school term ended. There was memory work for the program that was coming the last day of school. The children had painted attractive invitations to give to their parents, requesting their presence at the program.

The children were eager for the day when the report cards and prizes would be given out. A picnic lunch would be served at the schoolhouse, and there might be pie and ice cream!

On the other hand, it would not be all joy and happiness that day, for teacher would be leaving. She was going back to the "outside" world, from which she had come, back to the busy whirl of modern civilization, back to her own people. Sharna and LuDell knew both joy and sadness as they sat upon Lookout Rock one afternoon.

"I 'lows I'm going to miss 'er very much," said Sharna. "She 'as been kind and patient with us. Not many teachers would take us through two grades in one year. She 'as 'elped me in so many ways. I wish she didn't 'ave to go away."

"She'll miss all the picnics this summer," said LuDell. "We would 'ave so much more fun if she could go with us when we go inland by boat for our picnics. But I 'lows she will 'ave fun with 'er people when she gets back 'ome."

"Yes," agreed Sharna. "She 'as been away from them for a long time; I'm sure she will be glad to be 'ome again. I 'lows we won't 'ave any school next year. But I wish she would come back and be our teacher again."

"I do, too," said LuDell, gazing thoughtfully out over the sparkling water of the bay.

"She'll sail out beyond that gray line in a big boat, and we'll never see 'er again, never!"

"Oh, but we will," said Sharna. "If we love our heavenly Father and serve Him with all our 'earts, we'll see 'er again when Jesus comes. Teacher read it from the Bible. Don't you remember, LuDell?"

"Yes, I know," said LuDell solemnly.

Then came the long-expected day. Warm breezes blew across the bare rocks of the village. White birds hovered over the wharf to pick up the fish scraps that had been dumped into the water. They called to each other as they flew back and forth, or stood in groups, sunning themselves on the rocks along the shore. Bits of green were growing in the low marshy places between the rocks, for spring had come at last.

Everyone in the village was busy on this special morning. Faces were scrubbed, hair was neatly combed, and the best clothes were put on. This was the last day of school, and all the people of the village had been invited to the program at the schoolhouse on the hill. The boys brought extra chairs. The mothers brought good things to eat, and the fathers had been busy freezing and packing ice cream.

The girls came up the hill carrying the costumes that would be used in the plays. Sharna had helped to plan the simple costumes by following the pictures in teacher's books. She had selected costumes for the boys, too. Ken had helped by carving a long spear to be used in one of the scenes. He painted it with aluminum paint.

"Be careful," cautioned Sharna. " 'Old up that spear, Poggy. Don't let it drag in the mud!"

"I 'lows I'll be careful," said Poggy. "It will be thrown at me by King Saul when I play on David's 'arp."

At the appointed time the program began. It had been so well planned and rehearsed that teacher could sit back and watch with satisfaction. Don, the master of ceremonies, stood before the curtain and announced each number.

There were songs, recitations, exhibits, and short plays. How proud and pleased the parents were as each student did his part! Never before had they witnessed such a program as this. The teacher from "outside" had accomplished much this school term. She had done many wonderful things for their children. Perhaps, thought some of the parents, it would be a good idea for the children to attend high school.

Some of the parents had tried to persuade the teacher to come back for another school year; but every time they asked her, she had said her own people needed her, too.

There was a pause in the program while the scenery

was shifted behind the cotton curtain. When the curtain was pulled back, there appeared a dark cave. Lying near the entrance of the cave was Ken, who represented King Saul. While Verl read the Bible story, David and his men came out of the cave. Restraining his men from killing the king, David took his knife and cut away part of Saul's robe. Then he went away without harming the king.

Next came the scene where David played his harp before King Saul. Poggy, dressed in a striped toga, twanged on the rubber bands that had been stretched across a cardboard harp. Ken, dressed in a flowing robe, sat on a chair with a paper crown on his head. He held the glittering spear in his hand. As Verl read the passage of scripture, Poggy suddenly interrupted him by saying, "Wait a minute! I 'lows I'd better get out of 'ere before you throw that spear. I might get 'it!"

Don and Bobby quickly pulled the curtain. It was an unexpected ending to that scene!

After more songs and recitations, the girls presented a play about the life of Ruth and Naomi. Sharna never tired of listening while teacher read the beautiful story of the girl who loved her mother-in-law so much that she chose to accompany her to a strange land in order to serve God.

When the curtains opened, there was a country landscape with rocks, trees, blue sky, and a sandy path. LuDell played the part of Naomi, and Lolo was Orpah. Sharna took the part of Ruth. The teacher had arranged the conversation and the girls had memorized it. Dressed in their flowing garments, the girls played their parts well.

With clear voice, Sharna repeated slowly and very earnestly, "Entreat me not to leave thee, or to return from following after thee: for whither thou goest, I will go; and where thou lodgest, I will lodge: thy people shall be my people, and thy God my God: where thou diest, will I die, and there will I be buried: the Lord do so to me, and more also, if aught but death part thee and me."

At the thought of parting, Sharna looked at teacher. She found it hard to swallow the big lump that came up in her throat. Teacher noticed that Sharna was putting her heart into the play, and she turned away her face so that those sitting near her would not see her emotion.

When the curtains were drawn there was not a sound from the audience. Somehow the scene had gripped their hearts.

It was now time for teacher's part on the program. She arose and went to the front of the room. "My dear friends and pupils," she began, "it is with both joy and sadness that I speak to you. There is joy in anticipation of going back home and also in knowing that we have completed a successful school year. Yet there is sadness when I think of leaving you. I have grown to love all of you, and your kindness has been wonderful. I shall miss you more than I can say. But as we separate we can think of the day when there will be no more partings. Let us all be faithful to God and be ready to meet again in the beautiful home that is prepared for us."

Teacher began passing out the report cards to cover her emotion. There were several perfect papers that she had kept, as well as workbooks, flower booklets, scrapbooks, and paintings that the children had prepared during the year. These were passed out with the posters, basket craft, wood carving, and other busywork that the children had made.

"Tommy and Verl, you may take down the set of Japanese posters and distribute them," she said.

Then came the prizes. Each child received a token in appreciation for the splendid effort he had made.

"Sharna and LuDell have successfully completed the course of study for both grades 3 and 4," said teacher proudly. "To each of them I will give a special prize." The girls came forward and received packages. Sharna opened hers and took out a neatly bound copy of the Holy Bible.

"Thank you, teacher; thank you so much. Now I can learn to read it for myself."

LuDell had a similar prize, for which she was equally grateful.

"And Verl," said teacher, "since you had an unfortunate experience with your composition prize, I have another one for you." She handed Verl a box containing a pen and pencil set.

"Thank you," said Verl. "I 'lows I won't let the 'oodlums get these!"

"And Verl," she continued, "I know you will also appreciate this gift." She placed in his hands another box, a bit larger than the first. "It will be a comfort to you when you are lonely. It will guide you when the time comes for you to leave home; it will help you to know more about the heavenly Father we honor, worship, and trust. May He ever be your Guide and Counselor."

Verl opened the box to find a beautiful Bible. He looked at teacher and said, "I 'lows you gave me the best gift of all. I will read and study it, and keep it always. Thank you, teacher."

To each of the other children was given a copy of the New Testament. Some also received framed pictures to hang in their rooms at home, while others were given brightly colored mottoes and booklets of selected poems.

Good-by to Teacher

AS THE program ended, the schoolroom buzzed with conversation. Parents and friends complimented both teacher and pupils on the excellent program. "It was just grand," said Uncle Rex and Aunt Carol as they shook hands with teacher.

"Yes," said teacher, "the children have really done well. I'm proud of them. They worked hard to learn their parts, and I'm sure they feel now that it was worth all the effort they spent in preparation."

"My Bobby has always been so shy," said Bobby's mother. "It surprised me that he did so well."

"It was such a good program," said Uncle Tom and Auntie Lil. "You've done so much for the children."

"Thank you," said teacher softly.

"I want to tell you also," said Auntie Lil, "that we appreciate what you have done for us. You didn't know it, but it was through your influence that our daughter, Eulene, 'as come back to us. She's a changed girl—as she was before she went 'outside.' We want to make our 'ome a 'appy place so that she'll want to stay with us."

"Yes," added Uncle Tom, "you won't know the old 'ouse after I get it all painted."

Teacher smiled as she said, "I am sure it will look fine! But as for Eulene, I think a lot of the credit should be given to Sharna."

"Yes," said Auntie Lil, "but you told Sharna and the other children about God."

The minister shook hands with teacher. "A very fine program," he said sincerely. "Without a doubt the children have derived much good from the Bible stories they presented. It might be well for us to continue this in the future. May the bounties of the holy omnipotent Father be with you as you journey home."

"Thank you," said teacher. She shook hands also with the minister's wife.

Tommy's mother was standing by teacher's side. "You have helped my Tommy so much this year," she said earnestly. "He is a different boy. I used to fear he would turn out to be a hoodlum, but I'm not worried now."

"I'm so glad," said teacher. "Tommy is a fine boy."

"I don't see how you did it!' said Aunt Minnie, bubbling with enthusiasm as she shook hands with teacher. "I always wanted the children to sing together, but somehow I never did accomplish it. It was wonderful the way they sang and the way they played their parts. But, come, Uncle Joe wants to see you. He's sitting over there in his wheel chair."

Teacher followed Aunt Minnie over to greet Uncle Joe. He extended his hand in his usual friendly manner.

"I 'lows you 'ave done a lot for the young 'uns this

year, teacher." Uncle Joe heaved a big sigh as he added, "At least they'll amount to something when they grow big, and the credit will go to you."

"We can *all* have a little part in making an education possible for these children," said teacher, shaking hands with Uncle Joe.

Miss Arletta, who was standing near, said, "You've done a lot for Rocky Bay."

"And so have you, too, my dear," teacher replied.

"Oh, I can give simple medications and inoculations," said the nurse. "I can help bring new babies into the world and disinfect dog bites. But you have given the children a desire to further their education, to become useful in the world 'outside.' As Verl puts it, 'to learn 'ow to do it right.' "

"Thank you," said teacher humbly. "I had hoped to do just that. Thank you for your words of encouragement.

She turned to speak with Sharna's mother.

" 'Ow can I ever thank you for all you 'ave done for my children?" asked the woman.

"There is no need to thank me," said teacher. "It has been a privilege for me to help them."

"I 'lows we'll all miss you when you're gone. I 'ope you'll think of us now and then, and remember us in your prayers. We thank the heavenly Father for sending you to us. You've 'elped us far more than you'll ever know."

And so it went, all during the serving of the lunch. Even the children expressed their regrets because teacher was soon to leave them.

As LuDell and Sharna stood near eating their pie and

ice cream, LuDell said, "Every time we climb Lookout Rock and look across the bay, we'll think of you, teacher."

"Yes," said Sharna, " 'specially when the sun sets. Maybe someday we'll go 'outside,' too, after we finish the seventh grade. We want to go to high school and college and prepare to be teachers. Maybe someday we'll see you again. As Ruth said to Naomi, 'Whither thou goest, I will go: . . . thy people shall be my people, and thy God my God.' I am so glad you told us about the loving Father."

When the lunch was over, the mothers began gathering up the soiled dishes and silverware.

Teacher looked at her watch and said, "I think I will excuse myself. It will soon be time for the boat to leave."

Verl and Tommy were waiting for her near the door. "We'll carry your things down to the wharf for you," Verl offered. "We 'ate to see you go, though. I 'lows we'll never 'ave another teacher as good as you."

"Thank you, Verl; it's kind of you to say that. I consider it one of the nicest compliments I've ever received. Shall we go now?"

"Just a minute," said Verl. "I think grandfather and grandmother are going with us."

Soon Verl and Tommy were helping the elderly couple across the wind-swept rocks and down the path. Ken and Don soon joined them, for they, too, wanted to do something for the teacher, even if it were only to assist with her luggage.

As the boys made their way down the path with the trunk and other baggage, teacher turned to embrace grandmother and grandfather.

"Good-by, dears. You have been so kind to me during

my stay with you. I'll never forget you. May the Lord bless you both."

"Good-by," said grandmother. "You've been like a daughter to us. God grant you a safe journey."

"Amen," said grandfather solemnly.

When teacher and the boys reached the wharf, they found a group of villagers waiting. The last good-bys were said, and teacher stepped back for a moment. "I want to get the picture firmly in my mind. I want to remember all of you—just as you are. Don't forget, I love you very much."

Suddenly out of the group came Sharna. She put her arms around the teacher.

"I shall never forget you, Sharna," the woman whispered in her ear. "You are very precious to me. Let's trust in the heavenly Father. Then, when Jesus comes, we'll meet again. Good-by, Sharna." She kissed the girl on the cheek and held her for a moment. The whistle sounded as teacher walked up the gangplank.

As the boat pulled away from the wharf, teacher stood on deck waving good-by as long as she could see the group standing at the dock. She was glad to be on her way home, back to the rush and excitement of the city and the modern world. Yet she knew she was going to miss the simple life of Rocky Bay. She would miss the sea, the ever-blowing wind, the howling of the dogs, the bare rocks and hills, the cold, the snow, and the mud. She watched until the last faint outline of Lookout Rock disappeared from sight. "I shall miss them," she whispered; "but I 'lows most of all, I'll miss Sharna of Rocky Bay."

TEACH Services, Inc.
P U B L I S H I N G

We invite you to view the complete
selection of titles we publish at:
www.TEACHServices.com

We encourage you to write us
with your thoughts about this,
or any other book we publish at:
info@TEACHServices.com

TEACH Services' titles may be purchased in
bulk quantities for educational, fund-raising,
business, or promotional use.
bulksales@TEACHServices.com

Finally, if you are interested in seeing
your own book in print, please contact us at:
publishing@TEACHServices.com
We are happy to review your manuscript at no charge.